DEATHLY EVER AFTER

A POISON INK MYSTERY

BETH BYERS

SUMMARY

Georgette Dorothy Aaron has found her dream home, her dream village, and her dream husband. She and Charles purchase their house, move, and then discover all isn't as it seems.

Have they found *another* village with dark secrets? Is their happily ever after going to fade so soon? Will they be able to uncover what is happening or have they made a terrible mistake?

CHAPTER 1

The goddess Atë, mistress of mischief, had been concerned when her favorite human had left behind the ridiculous town of Bard's Crook. The fools who had been too blind to see their chronicler in their midst? It had given Atë sheer, unfettered delight to watch Georgette Dorothy Marsh observe their idiocy and turn it into 'fiction.'

When Georgette had gone to Bath, Atë had found comfort in throwing Georgette and Harrison, the blind-to-her-cleverness former lover together. The joy had only increased as Atë witnessed Georgette and Edna Williams cross paths. Both were overlooked women with the wit to see the murders happening around them while the constables had blithely carried on in their assumptions. It had been pure viewing joy. Atë would have eaten butter-covered popcorn if she'd possessed it in her high abode.

The town of Harper's Hollow had concerned Atë in the extreme when she'd turned her gaze upon it. She'd noted the small river running through the town. The cobblestone streets and the pretty little walks. Georgette was imagining idyllic, innocent afternoons with Charles in a row boat or a long ramble with Marian through those unfenced orchards where one could walk through without anger or upset from the owner.

Atë had seen the teashop, which had excellent tea—though not the quirky, delightful tea Georgette enjoyed—and Atë had known many an early morning ramble with the dogs would end with the girls lying outside the shop while Georgette enjoyed a scone with milky, sweet tea.

Atë admitted to herself that if she were Georgette she'd want to live in such a pretty, normal place. Then, however, Atë noticed the whispers of Georgette's neighbor, Miss Eckley, with her long-time friend, Miss Laurentis. They were whispering about the previous inhabitant of Georgette's house. The simple Polly Siegel who had disappeared between one fraught afternoon, a stormy night, and one dark morning. When Atë turned her gaze to the world to find Polly Siegel, Atë gasped in sheer, wonder-filled, cruel excitement. Oh, she thought viciously, this is going to be fun.

~

GEORGETTE DOROTHY AARON

"I have missed the dogs," Georgette told Charles, laying her head on his arm while he drove the auto. It was loaded with their baggage from the honeymoon and the things she'd bought while overseas. Tea. An excess of tea. Funny little fruit-flavored wines and cordials. An excess of chocolate along with an excess of tulip bulbs. It had been utterly delightful.

It wasn't the shopping, wandering in fields of flowers, or long mornings curled together in bed that had been so delightful. It was belonging to someone and having someone belong to her. If there was one thing that Georgette had learned to do all too well, it had been to be alone. Once she'd gotten past being with someone excessively, feeling smothered, and needing to press a kiss on his cheek and run from their hotel room alone, she'd gotten quite used to it. Having Charles was rather like having an attentive, comfortable coat.

She grinned at the idea and squeezed his fingers where they were tangled with hers. She had little doubt that she'd been as suffocating to him at times. In fact, when she'd reached her limit, she'd just said, "Charles, darling, I love you. But you must get away from me and let me write for an afternoon."

He'd stared at in her in shock, jaw dropped open, and then kissed her soundly on the mouth. "Oh thank heavens. The sound of your breathing is driving me mad."

Georgette did not take that personally. After all, if

he tapped his finger one more time against the back of his book, she was going to pull it from his hands and beat him about the head with it.

"I do love you," she told him seriously. Her gaze moved over his face, hoping she hadn't offended him. His eyes were crinkled with humor and his smile was quirked to the side as though he were both relieved and just a little snubbed. She took in his dark hair, the grey at his temples, the strong set of his shoulders, and she smiled tenderly. She *did* love him. She was just sick of him.

"I love you too." His head cocked at her and he grinned fiercely. "I don't want to see you for at least four hours."

"Perfect," she told him. "I'm going to write, have a tea all by myself, and read a French novel or something."

He laughed, kissed her again, and said, "I'll be at the pub smoking and having a pint."

Georgette didn't even look up when he left. She was too happy to sit down to her typewriter and get the story that had been itching at the back of her head started. Really, she thought, it should start with tulips.

Before, however, it started with tulips—she rang down to the front desk, ordered an excessive tea tray, opened the window to hear the sound of the passersby on the quaint Amsterdam road, and then took in a long, deep breath. Listen to that, she had thought with love, no tapping. No breathing. No shifting things about. No half-bored ideas of what they could do next. Georgette slowly let her breath out, sighed in joy, and then took her seat. She was gone to the world before the knock on the door with her tea and she stayed gone long past when Charles returned.

She didn't notice him, but he told her later he took note of her flying fingers and the publisher in him came out. He wrote her a note and disappeared until the husband in him returned, and then he pulled her from the typewriter and down to the restaurant. It was then they decided to head home.

Certainly, their house wasn't fully ready. They'd be living in a construction zone, but Georgette wanted nothing more than to feel at home again. After feeling outside of her skin in her cottage in Bard's Crook, then traveling to Bath where she'd been suffocated with too many Parkers, and then being on her honeymoon—Georgette desperately needed nothing more than her own space.

"Darling Georgie," Charles asked as he turned the auto onto the road that led into Harper's Hollow, "what are you dreaming of?"

"An office," she admitted. "A space that will be mine for writing. Maybe puttering in the garden. The dogs." She smiled when he lifted her hand to kiss it. "What are you dreaming of?"

"I'm rather more eager than I'd thought to return to work. I'm not sure I know how to not work most of the time. Will you be terribly upset if I half-neglect you?"

Georgette's lips spread into a slow smile and she told him seriously, "There is no one I want to be around more than you, but I think I might be a solitary creature by nature. If you need to work, as long as you promise to love me still, I will entertain myself and love you still."

"I promise to love you, darling. I suspect before long we'll rather be together than separate."

"It's just..."

"Yes..."

They laughed and then snuggled down for the drive. They had only Eunice to help them, Georgette thought, and the house was much larger than Georgette's little cottage and there was Charles too. Marian, Georgette suspected, would appear rather sooner than later.

Their house looked better when they arrived. A gothic masterpiece in its heyday, the house was four stories of dark grey stone. It had monstrous oak trees that were interspersed with stretches of grass and an occasional weeping willow.

When last Georgette had seen it the windows were dark and dirty. Now most of them shone with arched half circles above wide, tall rectangles. The broken window had been replaced and the rest had been cleaned. The grass had been cut and the bushes were trimmed and the good bones of the house reflected the care.

"This is where I say I told you so," she said as she climbed out of the auto. Georgette hadn't waited for Charles to open the auto door. Her dogs were in the yard—along with Marian's handsome fellow—and Georgette had kisses to receive. She was kneeling, getting her loves from the wriggling, low-whining dogs. She hadn't been aware that dogs could guilt you with the low whining they did when you returned until she'd been separated from her girls for a few days before Bath.

"This is where I say you were right," Charles said, leaning down to rub Susan's belly while Dorcas licked Georgette's face frantically. "Especially as we got it for a song."

"I assumed it must be you," Marian said from the steps up to the house. "I've just been exploring the updates without you. I'm not even a little bit sorry to have seen it first."

"You weren't first," Georgette told her, hugging her tightly. "The workers and Robert were."

Marian pursed her lips and scowled. "Even Joseph has seen it before me. He came down to help Robert with something while I had a dress fitting."

Georgette pulled away from Marian and said, "I missed you."

Georgette stepped inside and paused. She had *known*—simply known—this was the house. But her breath was caught as she stared. She didn't see any of the work yet to be done. She saw only the perfection of her house.

The hall had a parlor on either side. Just down the hall was a library on the left and an office on the right. It ended with a grand dining room, breakfast room, and the kitchens at the back of the house. They had been added later and were the first thing that Eunice had insisted on updating. The next floor had an office for the lady of the house. Eight bedrooms were found on the subsequent floors. The attics contained servants' rooms, storage, and the nursey which had long since given over to storage as well. The outline of the nursey could be seen amidst the old furniture, random trunks and boxes.

There was also a small bedroom off of the kitchens that Eunice had taken for her own. Over the stable-turned-garage was another set of servants' bedrooms that were entirely unused.

The house was old and had been well-loved until the last decade when it had stood empty and neglected, but it seemed her hopes that the neglect hadn't done permanent damage were answered.

"Robert said they just needed to clean and refinish the floors." Marian was watching Georgette, as was Charles. Both Marian and Charles seemed more interested in Georgette's reaction than the house itself.

"They're lovely." She had no idea what kind of wood they were, but it was dark with lovely shine and personality. She stared up at the new chandelier which —Robert had written—had been wired with light and updated.

"The whole house has been cleaned except for the cellars and attics," Marian said. "They repaired everything that had to be done before you could move in. Then Robert turned to the kitchens and the bathrooms. Little things like the heating and the water."

Georgette laughed at the expression on Charles's face. He'd moved from watching her to looking around. She guessed he was realizing that it was going to be a constant disturbance for quite some time.

"What have we done?"

"You'll see," she told him. "I love it already." Georgette hooked her arm through his and tugged him through the house. It was the first time she was seeing the inside, but that didn't matter. It had everything she had dreamed of when she'd dreamed of a house. If she'd made a list and asked God for it, the dreams couldn't have been fulfilled more perfectly. The light-filled library with the heavy bookcases, the large windows begging for window seats, the rolling ladder for the floor-to-ceiling bookcases. They were, she saw, still mostly full from whomever had lived here before.

Georgette merely glanced into the kitchens before leading Charles to his office. The list was going to be so fun to make, but she didn't expect Charles would enjoy the process nearly so much as she did. Instead she ordered him to tell her how he wanted it and she'd make it a priority.

She'd have to make her own office a priority, she thought. The only way they'd been able to buy this house was because the former owner had let it go for a song upon their low offer. Georgette grinned at Marian as she shut the door on poor, dazed Charles. Then she spun in a circle, feeling as though some god was looking down on her and grinning. This house—it was perfect. A dream. Everything she could have wanted, and if she had to write twice as fast to make the vision come alive, she would.

CHAPTER 2

GEORGETTE DOROTHY AARON

"Tell me everything," Georgette ordered. She had found Eunice in the back garden and squeezed her until shaken off. Once Eunice broke free, Georgette dragged her to the kitchens for some tea.

Eunice wouldn't just sit with them, but Georgette and Marian took a seat at the kitchen table while Eunice was happily making a plate of biscuits and tarts while she made the tea. It took mere minutes for Georgette to be sighing over her favorite tea with a raspberry tart in front of her and a lavender and sage butter biscuit waiting to be dunked in her tea.

"Mr. Charles's furniture was placed in a bedroom," Eunice told her. "Your bed was too small for a married couple. I ended up putting my old bed in the attic and taking yours. Georgette, the master bedroom was a mess. It needs more work than we could get done in time. We ended up just removing the scraps of furniture and garbage."

Georgette didn't care about that. Whatever room they started with would be fine until they finished fixing the master bedroom. In a house of this size, Georgette guessed the master was the huge bedroom that overlooked the back garden. It wasn't as though they had a tribe of children to house and needed every bedroom functional immediately. Though, she thought, happily, it might not be too long before they had one.

"No, no," Georgette muttered, shaking her head and glancing at Marian as if to ask if she could believe this nonsense. "Tell me of the wedding plans. The neighbors. Who shall I watch out for, who am I going to love, what is there to do? Have you tried the teashop?"

Eunice grunted. "You'd do better to focus on this house, Miss Georgie."

"Yes, Miss Georgie, turn your head to own roof." Marian's echo ended with a giggle.

"Speaking of roofs," Georgette said merrily, "tell me all about the hunt for yours."

"Joseph made an appointment to see one here," Marian said. "It's why I came down so early and am here, but he had to cancel."

"So you didn't see it?"

"He's not here," Marian sighed. "He had to call the local constable and request that they come by your house and tell me. They sent some boy. I only just found out that my plans for the day had come to another abrupt end."

"Well, let's go ourselves." Georgette had noted the 'another' and wondered if Marian was unhappy. Charles and Georgette had been gone for nearly a month, so it seemed all too possible that Marian's feelings for Joseph had...adjusted? Oh, how Georgette hoped not.

Marian stared at Georgette as if she had gone mad and then glanced at Eunice who lifted her brows. Eunice and Georgette had learned long ago to do for themselves without a man. It wasn't as though they couldn't nag Charles along with them. He wasn't officially due at the office until Monday, and it was only Friday morning.

"Get our hats, darling. Eunice, do you want to come lend your wisdom?"

"No," she said flatly. "I've had quite enough of looking at new houses. Besides, Mr. Joseph isn't a man who is going to give in to romantic ideas like Mr. Charles. If you like the place, tell him so. He'll look to ensure the roof and pipes and such are in order."

Georgette laughed at the look on Marian's face. With a quick draining of the tea and a popping of a biscuit into her mouth, Georgette smashed a crumby kiss on Eunice's cheek. "Missed you, darling. Come, Marian."

The dogs followed Georgette to Charles's office. She knocked and heard him call. He was standing on the ladder, pulling down the books from the previous occupant. "Look at this. These are ledgers for a business. I feel we should pack them up and send them on."

Georgette laughed at the deep frown. "They did know they were selling the house with the contents. Surely whoever sold this house knew what they were letting go of?"

"We should at least see if the business is still running, darling. If it is, they might need these."

"I'll take care of it. Stack them here." She gestured to an empty corner. "Come, dearest, we're going with Marian to see a possible house."

He blinked in question.

"Joseph has a case and cannot get away," Georgette explained. "We're going to tell him whether it's worth coming down for another look."

"We set our wedding date," Marian announced.

Georgette squealed and waited for the date with bated breath.

"Which Joseph told Charles. Look at his face," Marian added. Charles was indeed grinning without surprise.

Georgette gasped, smacking Charles on the shoulder. "Secret keeper."

"Marian wanted that delightful—yet high-pitched —reaction." Charles laughed at Georgette's gasp. Laughing harder still when she snapped her mouth closed.

"My parents are insisting we find a place to live before it comes to pass. We set the date, but they are saying it can't go through if we haven't bought a house and outfitted it, and the wedding is *only* three months to go. I should like to have the house immediately since my mother will probably interfere with every step of outfitting it."

"Or you could live in a half-finished, still-filled-with-garbage home," Georgette reminded her. "Or you could be newlyweds on a long distance ramble with a two-man tent. Or you could stay with us."

Marian gasped and shuddered. "I keep dreaming we don't find a place. I get dressed for the wedding, but my father refuses to walk me down the aisle. I get married anyway, and my mother is wailing. Not the normal tears mothers cry when a child marries, but as though I had been murdered in front of her."

"That is disturbing," Georgette said. "I recommend eloping."

Marian continued. "During the toasts at the wedding breakfast, people talk about how foolish we are and no one throws rice and then Joseph is called away to solve a crime and I'm all alone on the stairs and my mother tells me, 'I told you so.'"

"Well, this is all easily solved. We'll go look at the house with you, and Charles will shackle himself to Joseph on the big day. Charles," Georgette said stridently, "we need you."

Charles stared in alarm.

"All you have to do is lend your manly presence."

"My manly presence?"

"Whoever the fellow is with the house to sell, you can be sure he won't take us seriously. If you come, he'll ignore us and we can decide."

"You decide?"

"Marian."

"Marian?"

"Charles darling, it isn't so important what Joseph thinks about the place. Not really. He'll be off at work while Marian will be wiping faces and listening to tantrums in those kitchens. She needs to love it more than anyone else does. Joseph has to like it a little. Marian has to love it."

"Ah." Charles cleared this throat and adjusted his coat. "I can lend you my manly presence then. Just this once." The last was said with a wink.

Georgette patted his cheek and added, "We'll leave you at the pub on the way back, shall we?"

His face brightened.

"You can talk the most recent sports whatnot and have your pipe and Marian and I will quite happily discuss paint colors."

Charles nodded and handed Georgette a list. "For the office. I think I shall have to be working in London until it's well done."

Georgette stuck it carefully in her handbag and then grinned at Marian. They made their way to the auto and Charles listened to Marian's directions to the office of the man who was supposed to show them the house. Charles went inside and got him while Georgette climbed into the back of the auto with Marian.

"Are you upset Joseph isn't here?"

"It's more the flavor of things to come, do you know?" Marian shrugged and then said rather seriously, "I fell in love with a detective, Georgie. He isn't going to have more regular hours or even an idea of when things might go mad. I can either get upset about it and be upset simply all the time, or I can be grateful that a good man loves me." She hooked her arm through Georgette's and added, "I've made him promise that I can always have a dog or two and that we could live near you. I also told him if he ever missed my birthday, anniversary, or the birth of a child, I'd never let him hear the end of it."

Georgette hid the rush of emotion. Live near Georgette? They had spoken of it, but in a distant sort of manner. To hear it declared outright was over-whelming. Her heart was flooding, but she held it back when Charles and the man of business arrived. She bit down on her lip and listened as Charles conversed with Mr. Stripes about Harper's Hollow. It turned out that this fellow had helped with the sale of their new house.

"Ah, yes," Charles said, with a cultured tone he'd never used with her.

It was an unconscious switch, she thought, but he'd adjusted his attitude. He seemed almost above her when he spoke like that. She glanced at Marian who had noted the change and was watching Georgette.

Did Marian think that Charles was too good for her? No, of course not. Marian wasn't like that. Marian would never assume Georgette wasn't good enough for anyone at all. Not even because Georgette was a village old maid who hadn't had the courage to tell her own stories at first.

She shook off the idea almost immediately. She deserved better than to see herself in that manner, and quite frankly—Charles deserved better of her. She loved him. She was, in fact, besotted with him. Like a girl in a fairy tale. She might not have thrown herself into his arms after that first offer, but she might have been convinced.

Georgette scoffed quietly. When she'd first met Charles, Georgette had been so desperate that she would have thrown herself into his arms at the slightest chance he was in earnest. Georgette had only hesitated when he finally did offer because she'd become something she'd never thought she'd be.

Independent.

It seemed that when you were uncertain where your next meal was coming from or how to keep your house, you couldn't think beyond those things. Once you were fed and housed? Well, anything was possible, wasn't it? You could dare to wish for something more than a—than a—rescue from Jane Austen's Mr. Collins.

Georgette was pulled from her thoughts by the little house where they arrived. Marian frowned in confusion, which caused Georgette to frown. Despite whatever was wrong with this house, Georgette loved it. It was a small, stone house, reasonable in its size and adorable, like a fairytale cottage sized up.

The fencing around the property was stone and there was an excess of fruit trees. Summer would be arriving in mere days, and the trees were a fairy wonderland. There was a small stone shed behind the house that matched it almost exactly.

Marian was nodding as she stared.

"I know that Mr. Joseph Aaron said he wanted something quite close to the train station," the man of business said. "He gave me a very precise list, and this isn't the house we were supposed to visit today. But it is also quite within the budget he set. The previous owner was a sweet little lady. She decided to move in with her older children after, well—" He shrugged. "Her children took good care of her. She wants it sold, she wants to be rid of it. The price reflects her desire to just be done."

"What is different about the house from what Joseph wanted?" Charles asked.

The man listed things which, in Georgette's opinion, were entirely without value.

"If this isn't what Joseph wants," Charles began, but Marian grabbed Georgette's hand.

"It can't hurt to look, darling," Georgette told him. She stepped out of the auto and approached the house, knowing Charles would indulge her. Marian hurried after, grabbing Georgette's hand.

"What is the most appealing for you, I think"—Mr. Stripes glanced at Georgette and Marian, noted their clutched hands, and nodded at them—"is that there is a quite easy walk from your house to this house. You see, here? Your property runs up against a wood. This property runs up against the same wood. There's a lovely little walk between the houses. A faster walk, in fact, than a drive, as it would be necessary to motor around the entire wood."

Mr. Stripes opened the door to the cottage, and they all stepped inside.

Georgette had little doubt, given the stars in Marian's eyes, that her friend was seeing the same things Georgette had when she'd first seen her house. Marian was imagining future children playing in the garden, walks between the two houses, a Christmas tree just there, with a wreath on the door.

Charles hesitated and Georgette lifted her brow at him. He smiled at her and let go of whatever objections he possessed. Together, they trailed Marian through the house. It was a snug place. A parlor, quite nice kitchens, an office, and three bedrooms with a roomy attic. The furniture was still in place, covered in sheets.

"The furniture is included in the purchase," Mr. Stripes said smoothly when Marian lifted one of the sheets and ooohed. "It isn't the same, you know, for the row house. That will allay the price quite a bit, making it a much better purchase for an initial outlay. Everything you see here—"

Marian's gaze had fixed on the dark, shining wood of the sideboard in the dining room. "I'd like to walk it again. Without you, Mr. Stripes. I need to—"

She didn't elaborate on what she wanted, just nodded pleasantly and left him behind.

Marian walked it a good half-dozen times before Mr. Stripes offered to let them have the key until Joseph arrived. "I suppose I can trust a Yard man, and I do know where you live."

His laugh was a ho-ho-ho and as Charles walked him to the auto to take him back to his office, Georgette turned to Marian and demanded, "Did you hear his laugh?"

"Hmmm?" Marian had taken off one of the sheets and was trying out a large, overstuffed chair in the corner.

No doubt, Mr. Stripes was quite hopeful he'd made a sale. He had if Georgette was a judge of the matter.

Joseph might have given Mr. Stripes a quite reasonable list, but he'd give Marian whatever she wanted, and Georgette had little doubt Marian was rocking her babies in her imagination. Dreaming of making a Christmas roast, of watching first steps happen under that apple tree. Georgette left Marian to it and left the house to step into the wood. The path Mr. Stripes had described was just as he said. A bit of a ramble through a lovely wood, and they'd be able to have a morning tea together.

Georgette walked back towards the house while Marian stepped outside once more.

"I love it," Marian said.

"I can tell," Georgette replied. "It's wonderful."

"Do you think he'll let me have it?"

Georgette laughed. "I think he'd let you have anything he could give you. He's utterly your captive. Also, he cancels on you so often, he has a well of guilt that you can draw upon whenever you desire something."

Marian smiled, but her eyes were already far away again. She was bouncing on her toes and then muttered, "My parents will insist on seeing it and casting judgement. They'll see that window that needs

to be replaced and the fact that it's a bit older and—"
Marian made a sour face as Charles returned to the
house.

"Or," Georgette said kindly while Charles came
toward them, "you could tell your parents you're going
to buy the row house, but that you're intrigued by this
snug little cottage. Lead them to insist Joseph buy you
the house you were going to buy all along."

"Or," Charles suggested smoothly, appearing in the
doorway. His voice was back to its normal tone. It was
gentle, she thought. He spoke to her always with an
edge of gentleness, and she'd never noticed. She
tangled their fingers together while Charles finished.
"You could do what you both want, as you are adults,
and your parents don't get to weigh in on everything
you do. Sooner or later, you have to stop them from
making your choices."

"If you don't," Georgette said, envisioning a terrible
future, "they'll keep running over your plans with
their own demands. Marry when you want, buy the
house you want, and tell them you love them often.
They do love you."

"I am rather lucky to have them, aren't I?" Marian
smiled and kissed Georgette's cheek. "This is it,
Charles. Have I gone mad?"

"I like it," Charles said. "It's far more reasonable
than our monstrosity."

"But it doesn't have enough room for our books,"
Georgette reminded him. "We had to make a different
decision."

"You've got me there, darling."

CHAPTER 3

GEORGETTE DOROTHY AARON

Joseph arrived that evening and Marian dragged him out of Georgette's house to see the one she had her heart set on. He had a look on his face that said he knew was going to give in, and wasn't sure it was wise.

Charles, it seemed, agreed because called after them. "Just give it to her, Joseph. It isn't nearly as bad as this thing. Also, Marian will be wiping faces and dealing with your son's tantrums in the house. You should make sure she loves it."

Georgette elbowed him lightly to his shout of laugher. He trailed his fingers along her neck as the dogs chased after Joseph and Marian.

"There is a lot to do for this place, Georgette. The

whole top floor is full of, from what I can tell, a full century of garbage."

"It's going to be lovely when we're done," Georgette replied. Joseph and Marian were out of sight, so she turned to face him, sliding her arms around his waist. "You're going to spend the rest of our decades—once it's done—telling me how right I was."

"If I say it now, may I avoid the lifetime of I told you so's? The house has good bones. What's been redone is lovely. I can see a future here, Georgette, and I like it."

Georgette's teasing smirk told him no he was not going to escape the I-told-you-so's.

He tried, "I did agree and buy it."

"You just wanted me out of Bath before someone else turned up dead."

"No," Charles countered, "I wanted you in my arms and home where you belong. The rest was just fluff."

"I wouldn't have kicked up a fuss if you'd bought another house." It was easy to say when he'd bought the house she wanted. "Something like Joseph and Marian's house would have been fine."

He grinned at her, noting she'd already named the house his nephew's. She wasn't wrong, however, so he didn't counter her. Instead he pressed his lips lightly on hers. "I didn't want you to pass by this house for the rest of our decades and think about what could have been."

"I wouldn't have," Georgette told him seriously. "I would have been happy wherever we landed."

"Then, I suppose I didn't want to pass by this house

and wonder what would have happened if I'd been entirely insensible and foolish and bought it."

Georgette let her hands fall from his waist to his hands, keeping herself pressed against him. She tangled their fingers together as she daringly pressed up on her toes and kissed him. "I love you, Charles Aaron."

"And I you, Mrs. Aaron." He kissed her again and again until they heard the barking of the dogs and realized that quite a lot of time had passed while they were behaving as school children, stealing kisses before they were caught.

"Well?" Charles asked as they saw the shadows of Marian and Joseph appear. The dogs had already reached Charles and Georgette, circled them, and then run joyously back to the other couple. They darted back and forth without regard to the darkness. Georgette didn't disagree.

The way the moon shone overhead seemed to demand that everyone enjoy a nightcap and a smoke. Georgette followed Charles inside and then gasped when she saw that the tea tray had a lovely butter cake with chocolate ganache. It was her very favorite treat, and she had little doubt it was Eunice's way of saying she was grateful they were back together.

The tea was Georgette's favorite mix of cocoa beans, coffee beans, and tea. Odd and amazing, especially when you added an excess of sugar and milk. Joseph chuckled at Georgette's tea and then poured himself and Charles a cognac. Marian, on the other hand, decided to try one of Georgette's sweet cordials she'd purchased while she was on her honeymoon.

They lingered together for a while and then Charles pulled Georgette with him. It was the first night in their own house, and somehow Georgette was as nervous as she had been on her wedding night.

AT BREAKFAST, Georgette and Marian sipped tea without regard for the food. Georgette had learned to turn away when Charles ate breakfast. It wasn't that he shoveled it in like a school child with a fervor and utter lack of manners. He was quite polished in all he did. He opened the paper, drank his coffee, and quite reasonably worked his way through a loaded plate of eggs, bacon, tomatoes, and toast.

It was just that Georgette didn't like anything in her stomach until the tea had hit and somehow settled things. The sight of a feast before her stomach had decided it would accept food turned her body rebellious.

Therefore, Charles tucked his plate behind his newspaper, and Georgette sipped her tea, leaned back, eyes closed, while she considered upon the day. She wasn't functioning before tea, so her desire to consider upon the day was—instead—encompassed by revisiting the shreds of her dreams she could still remember, the theory that she needed a new pair of shoes, and the desire for a quite dashing black dress.

When Georgette reached for a piece of toast,

Marian said, "Oh good. I was wondering if you'd like to walk the house with me again today. Joseph is going to talk to Mr. Stripes. I have refused to give up my key."

"Yes," Georgette agreed instantly. "If you'll walk this one with me, the painter is coming just after lunch, and I feel like I must decide what he's going to do as soon as he's done with Charles's office."

They grinned at each other and then glanced towards their Aaron men, only to see each of them smiling a little indulgently at them. Georgette immediately rolled her eyes at Charles and he winked.

Joseph, however, seemed to have caught Marian's gaze. It turned almost lascivious with wanting and Georgette ended up standing and asking, "Would anyone else like a refill?"

Her question snapped the two lovers out of their silent desire-filled stare. Marian shook her head and glanced down at her cup while Joseph cleared his throat. "I really must be going if I'm going to speak to Mr. Stripes before I go into the Yard. Much to do and all that."

When he left, followed by Marian, Charles laughed wickedly. A moment later, he told her, "You don't need to start with my office.'

"I do, though," Georgette countered, filling his coffee, and returning to her toast and the seat by his side. "If your sanctuary in construction zone is what it should be, the rest of the process can be lingered over while I get it right. It won't be fun for you, but I'll enjoy it."

Charles examined Georgette and then said, "I would prefer if you focused on the master bedroom after my office. Did you see it? It's as if someone went mad in there. Or perhaps a duo of wild dogs took up residence. They'll have to replace plaster before they paint and possibly the flooring. It's a large job."

Georgette nodded and said, "Plan number one—darling Charles's office."

Charles snorted at the 'darling.'

"Plan number two—our bedroom."

He sniffed but didn't argue. Her grin was the wicked when she added, "Plan number three—if I'm not incorrect—the nursery."

It took Charles a moment to register what she'd said. His head cocked and his brow furrowed. His gaze moved over her, landing on her stomach. To be honest, it was quite a bit rounder than it had been when he'd met her, but it had been concave and starving then. Now, she just had a bit of outward curve that couldn't be called fat. He stared at her stomach for far too long for such an educated man and then repeated—rather like a hoarse toad, "The nursery?"

"Yes," Georgette said. "It's early days yet, but I always have been quite regular. I suppose anything could happen."

His skin had paled, and he set his coffee cup down with a tremble, making it clank against the saucer. "The nursery."

"Early days yet," Georgette told him. "I believe it's rather common for there to be issues with the baby

27

before you're very far along. Perhaps this one won't settle well."

He'd turned and pressed his hand against her forehead as though she might have a fever instead of being with child. "Baby."

Georgette nodded, letting his hand linger on her forehead.

"My heavens," he said and pulled her onto his lap. He leaned forward, once he had her situated, letting his head land on her chest. "Baby."

It was another hoarse whisper and Georgette couldn't quite tell how he felt. She wasn't worried. She had that list he'd made when he was still trying to get her to agree to marry him. It was engraved on her heart.

It read:

-Convince Georgette I love her.

-Convince Georgette to marry me.

-Convince Georgette to find a house for us.

-Find a house with

-an office so I can work from home at least half the time

-an office for Georgette so she can write dozens more books

-room for children

-room for too many books and more to come

-a garden for smoking pipes in

-a village that has an excellent pub

-create a happily ever after?

-convince Georgette to share her troubles

-convince Georgette to find a village that will work for Joseph and Marian as well

. . .

REALLY GEORGETTE THOUGHT, she felt as though she could adjust that list quite nicely to:

-Convince Georgette I love her.

-Convince Georgette to marry me.

-Convince Georgette to find a house for us.

-Find a house with

-an office so I can work from home at least half the time

-an office for Georgette so she can write dozens more books

-room for children

-room for too many books and more to come

-a garden for smoking pipes in

-a village that has an excellent pub

-create a happily ever after?

-convince Georgette to share her troubles

-convince Georgette to find a village that will work for Joseph and Marian as well

HIS LIST WOULDN'T HAVE REFERRED to children if he didn't want them. The sudden burden of one, however, might be more than he could handle without a few minutes. She let him lay his head on her chest and think while she played with his hair. All that was left was to create their happily ever after. That wasn't something they could cross out.

It was a process—a journey. If being single and alone for so long had taught Georgette anything, it had taught her that happiness was made in decision after decision and the attitudes you kept with those decisions.

You decided to be happy about having milk for your tea. Happiness was when you found puppies and loved them. It was made when you dared to trust and love another. Happiness was made when you had an issue—like being sick of your beloved's presence—and admitting it and working through it. Happiness was wanting what you had and working for what you wanted with an emphasis on enjoying the current.

"I'm going to meet with the fellow coming, Georgette." Charles stood, lifting her and setting her back on her own chair as though she weighed nothing. "I'll walk through the house again and make note of all the structural things. Darling, you choose the paint. Do you want the children in the attics?"

Georgette shook her head.

"Then we'll turn one of the larger bedrooms into a nursery. Or perhaps two. I think, if we have more than one, they'd rather be together, don't you? I always wished for that."

"I did too," Georgette admitted.

For a moment, their younger selves seemed to peek out from behind their eyes and greet the other. Lonely children that had found happiness in books. It was one of those things they'd discovered on their honeymoon. The fact of their solace in books had been obvious upon reflection.

Georgette hadn't had any siblings. Charles had two, but he'd lost one, and the other lived in the Caribbean Islands of all places. He'd been so much younger than his brothers that they'd been at school long before he was born.

"I can take care of it," Georgette told Charles. "It isn't like I can't ask you for help if I'm uncertain of what to do."

"I'll do it," Charles said. "This work is going to be done before you can't see your feet."

Georgette's gaze narrowed at that idea, and Charles's shout of laughter brought Marian back into the breakfast room. Charles raised an inquiring brow and Georgette shook her head. No, Marian didn't know. Georgette wanted to keep it between them for a while, and Charles understood for he said nothing.

CHAPTER 4

GEORGETTE DOROTHY AARON

he teashop was not what dreams were made of if they were being dreamed by Georgette. It was quaint, it had pretty little teapots. The baked goods smelled like they'd been made by angels. The woman who seated Georgette and Marian had been utterly delighted to meet a new resident and a future resident. She'd bustled over with a teapot.

It was filled with a quiet delightful lapsang souchong. Georgette added too much milk, to the lifted eyebrows and then hastily slapped on smile of Bernadette Coach. Mrs. Coach upgraded their requested plates of scones to a tiered offering with petit fours, biscuits, tarts, and scones. It did not, however, have odd little teas with the scent of coffee or the combination of cocoa and coffee. Georgette would endeavor to persevere.

Mrs. Coach then lingered long enough for Marian to say, "Oh, Mrs. Coach, do you have the time to sit with us? I confess, we're rather desperate to hear about Harper's Hollow. Especially since it's so—"

"Oh, dear, call me Bernadette. It is rather dreary and empty in here, isn't it? We've a bit of an outbreak, you know?"

"Outbreak?" Georgette demanded.

"Scarlet fever," Bernadette said. "It's the most terrible thing, you know. I fear that Dr. Fowler told poor Mrs. Halpert that her Jimmy had chicken pox."

Georgette blinked as she tried to file the names away. Getting gossip about people you didn't know was so much more work.

"Only—" Marian asked.

"It was scarlet fever! All of Mrs. Halpert's children have it. She has seven children, you know. And Mrs. Smitty brought her children over to expose them to chicken pox while school was out of session. Only— well, now they have scarlet fever too."

"Oh my goodness," Marian gasped. "Oh how horrible."

Georgette's jaw had dropped open. She was mostly sure that she was growing a baby, and never had she felt such an instant certainty that if it had been her children, she might have run Dr. Fowler down in Charles's auto for making such a mistake. To have *all* your children get such an illness! It was the worst thing Georgette had ever heard.

"Can we do anything for them?" Georgette asked, her mind still on her own baby. She'd had scarlet fever as a child, but had Charles?

Georgette sipped her really very excellent tea with disappointment and listened to Bernadette gossip for a good quarter of an hour before the woman asked, "Now where do you live?"

"We bought a rather old, large house that was quite rundown. I'm not sure if it had a name. Nor, to be honest," Georgette admitted, "am I sure of who owned it before. It's on Persephone Street."

"Oh," Bernadette said carefully. There was something in that *oh*, but whatever gossip went with Georgette's house was not revealed. Georgette kept her smile even though she very much wanted to cross-examine the woman until she revealed the secrets of Georgette's house.

"And you, my dear?"

"We haven't purchased one yet," Marian said. Her gaze was searching, but Bernadette didn't pick up on the opening to discuss whatever there was to know about Georgette's house.

"Where are you looking, my dear?"

Marian shrugged as she lied, "We're still deciding and really, Joseph does prefer to make that decision. I'm sure wherever we choose will be lovely. What can you tell us about the history of Georgette's house? Were many children raised there?"

"Oh certainly since it was built," Bernadette said, succumbing to the direct question. "I'm afraid the last owner didn't have any children of his own. His wife died rather suddenly, and he left Harper's Hollow. I don't know if he ever remarried, but I doubt a child has lived in that house since—well, since, Victoria was queen."

"Really?" Georgette gasped. "Has it been empty so long?"

"Oh no," Bernadette shook her head. "The last mistress died. Oh, I don't know? A few years ago. Perhaps as many as five. It was just the two of them and their housekeeper for years before she died."

Georgette felt certain that there was more to the story. Once again, she glanced at Marian and then they finished their tea and left Bernadette to her shop.

"Someone was captured and held captive in your house," Marian announced as they walked towards Georgette's home.

"Maybe the last person died there."

"You'd expect that," Marian said with a scoff, "in a house that old. Dozens have probably died there."

"That seems an excessive number."

Georgette's mouth twisted. Marian wasn't wrong. The house was so old it had both a music room and a billiards room. There was no question that people had died there many times over the course of its life.

"Maybe the people who lived there before were criminals."

Marian shook her head and they hooked arms. "Either way, I do love your house. It's like—this will sound silly."

"Tell me anyway," Georgette ordered.

"Well, it's like in Bard's Crook, you were like your

cottage. You were little, quaint and overlooked. Did you see how she treated you? Bernadette Coach treated you like a real person. Now, you're like your house. You aren't going to get away with being overlooked anymore. I wager you'll hate it half the time."

"Well yes," Georgette agreed. "All I really wanted was a few people. I have that now. Charles and you. The dogs."

"That doctor though," Marian exclaimed. "Can you imagine? We need to stop by the vicar and send something to that poor suffering family. I won't be using that Dr. Fowler, I can tell you that. Thankfully London is so close. It won't be all that hard to get someone to look after us who *isn't* Dr. Fowler."

Georgette blinked very rapidly and knew that she was either going to take a suite in London when her baby was expected or she was going to see if Harper's Hollow had more than one doctor. Perhaps Charles could persuade one to set up shop here. After misdiagnosing those children, Georgette and Marian couldn't be the only ones who didn't want Dr. Fowler near their children.

They walked to the vicar and spoke to him, introducing themselves. Their offering was taken so gratefully, Georgette immediately followed up with a duplication of it for a few days later. Especially when he said that little children were suffering and all they could be persuaded to eat was broth and fresh fruit. Broth and fresh fruit, Georgette thought, they would have.

They passed three teenagers in the garden. They

were sitting together in an unmoving row, and Georgette wanted to give them a cricket bat and a ball.
They really did look as though they needed sleep,
food, and exercise.

They reached the house just as the men who had
been hired to fix it were leaving with Charles walking
them out. He hooked Georgette's hand and they left
Marian as Charles told Georgette what he'd ordered.
She nodded, without objections, and then revealed her
afternoon.

"Something about our house?" he asked when she
told him of Bernadette's cagey reply. "The last family
living here was probably unmarried or something,
darling. Nothing to worry over."

"Oh, I'm not worried," Georgette confessed, "I'm
curious. I am, however, worried—" She told him of the
doctor, the sick children, and the donations.

"Yes, yes, whatever those children need. My heavens, Georgette, we must find another doctor for you."

"I was thinking just the same thing," Georgette
confessed, telling him of her rage for her baby who
was just an idea at the moment. A real child? One in
her arms? One she'd longed for years? Georgette could
not imagine any greater horror than the ones poor
Mrs. Halpert and Mrs. Smitty were facing. All their
children sick with an illness that could kill or maim
them.

They circled their garden and Charles lit his pipe
while Marian had gone for the dogs. They were
chasing around the green as Marian passed through
the back gate with a wink and wave. Georgette noted

the pad of paper in Marian's hands and guessed that her friend was going to make the list of what she wanted to do to her own house alone. Should Georgette chase after her?

No, she thought, it was just before teatime and Charles would soon be at work during these hours. She wanted to spend the day with him as much as she could. It didn't matter that she'd gotten sick of him on their honeymoon, she was going to miss him once he was back in the office more.

They walked through the house again with Charles explaining what he'd ordered. He'd left all of the paint, carpeting, and papering to her and ordered only the necessary repairs that would return a room to functional if somewhat hideous. He had, in fact, taken away all the things she hadn't really wanted to do and left her with the fun part of turning their house into something more.

The master bedroom would be repaired first and then they'd remove the wall from the room that Charles and Georgette were currently using, and prepare it for a nursery. "I thought this one," Charles explained, "because the windows let in so much light. It seems like a happy place, but we can change it to another pair of rooms if you desire?"

Georgette shook her head. He'd chosen perfectly, and she was unsurprised. As they discussed colors for the walls and things to buy their baby, they heard the dogs return. Marian returned, but she was met in the garden by Joseph. Georgette and Charles watched from the upper window as Marian squealed and threw herself in Joseph's arms.

"Their offer on that house must have been accepted," Charles told her.

She grinned at him and then said, "You know, she'll be here all the time."

"Her children and ours will play together. It will be like we had a dozen children without actually having to feed, raise, and educate a dozen."

Georgette laughed, and they joined their friends for a late tea. Marian needed to return to her parents' home in London that night but would be back for the next weekend when Joseph would also be able to join them, barring issues with a case. He intended to move into the house as soon as his offer was officially accepted, as Mr. Stripes had said he didn't believe the owners would mind if Joseph took early possession.

Georgette curled her fingers through Charles's as they watched their friends leave. It would be an often thing, she thought, in this happily ever after they were creating. Only, in the future, they'd be walking Joseph and Marian to the back gate, knowing they'd be finding their way through the wood, through their own back gate, and into the snug little house that would soon be theirs.

CHAPTER 5

GEORGETTE DOROTHY AARON

Georgette escaped her house four days later when the sound of the pounding hammer had driven her quite mad. She'd been trying to write while the workmen came and went, but Charles had paid them to work quickly. A team had come and worked on the master bedroom and the new bath while Georgette had tried and failed to write for days.

Could she, she wondered, write at the local library? Or perhaps at one of Bernadette's back tables? The master bedroom was being papered with maroon paper, striped with silver. The stripes were a bare pin's width and subtle in the extreme. The floor had already been refurnished and Charles's furniture was more than adequate for her wants. It was a large bed with a heavy carved frame. The only thing she'd done was buy new bedding that matched the maroon of the walls.

The bedroom had two dressing rooms off of it with room for plenty of clothes. Charles, to Georgette's delight, had filled his completely. She, on the other hand, had a few dresses, blouses, and jumpers. She hadn't taken up even a quarter of her dressing room. Charles had taken one look at her closet, cursed, and told her to go shopping.

Georgette had, however, reminded him that she'd had better wait until her body changed. He shook his head, muttering that he hadn't realized she'd brought her *entire* wardrobe on their honeymoon.

The bath was not finished as quickly. A plumber had to come in and lay the piping which had been done at the outset, let alone having to wait for the bathtub they'd ordered which was weeks out. They wouldn't be able to truly finish things as quickly as Charles had desired, but they would be able to sleep in their room that evening.

Georgette walked towards the center of the town. Perhaps she'd take her paper and pencils and sit next to the little river. She stopped by the teashop and had them make her a pot of tea, enjoying the mutter of conversation while she sipped her tea.

She heard something about the "old Essent place," but didn't realize it was her house until she glanced up rather unconnected to anything the other women were saying and realized they sputtered to a stop. Georgette smiled with that dull, slow smile she'd used for years before Charles came along, and then sipped her tea and sighed.

Why didn't they just introduce themselves? Why didn't *she* just introduce herself? She frowned, mouth twisting, and wondered if she were an utter fool for not speaking up. Finally, she finished her tea and took her leather bag, placing its strap over her body.

As she left, she said, "Hello. I know it's very forward, but I'm afraid I'm new in town."

"Oh hello," one of the women said. She had a good five years on Georgette along with several stone. Neither of which would have bothered Georgette, but the woman also had snake eyes. "So nice to meet you. I'm Carolyn Holmes."

Georgette touched hands with the woman as she said, "Georgette Aaron."

Her gaze turned to the second woman who wasn't so fleshy, so old, or so mean-faced. "Laura Holmes."

"We've married brothers," Carolyn told Georgette. "I understand you're newly married."

"Indeed, I am." Georgette smiled and the memory of her joy flooded her.

"A bit old to be a newlywed."

"Indeed it is." Georgette refused to let the snide tone bother her or steal her happiness. "How fortunate I am to have fallen quite so thoroughly in love despite my age. I have come to believe, however, that one can fall in love at any age."

"Do you really think so?" Carolyn glanced at Laura as if to ask if she could believe this nonsense.

"Oh I think so," Laura said, ignoring Carolyn's cold glance. "After all, I do love Donald rather a lot. I suspect I'll love him even when I'm eighty, should I live so long."

"Exactly, my thought." Georgette met Laura's gaze with a bright, winning grin that had won over Charles, Marian, and anyone else with the wit to see the charm in her smile.

"You bought the old Essent place?" Carolyn demanded.

"If that is the rather rundown old charmer on Persephone Street, then yes. That was Charles and I."

"And I heard a rumor that the old Siegel house was purchased as well?"

"Well, I don't know. I'm afraid I'm rather unfamiliar with the old names that people use for houses in this village. I'm afraid that I've only lived here for a few days."

"She means," Laura said kindly, "the little house that is connected through the wood to the Essent—well your house."

"Oh yes," Georgette nodded. "My husband's nephew and my dear friend have purchased the home. They'll be married soon, so you'll be seeing Joseph Aaron dashing to the train here and there rather soon, I think. But Marian will be a few more months before she moves along."

"Interesting." Carolyn's tone was weighted. "You

know, of course, the rumors about those *particular* houses?"

Georgette couldn't possibly know, and Carolyn knew it. Mean women. Georgette never understood why they needed to belittle others. Laura sighed. It was a quiet rebellion, but Carolyn heard and shot Laura a rather terrifying look.

Laura, however, continued in her rebellion. "How could she, Carolyn dear? Mrs. Aaron didn't even know that her house was owned by Theodore and Yelena Essent."

"What a delightful name," Georgette said blithely, knowing that neither woman felt the same. She adored the disgusted look that came onto Carolyn's face, while Laura didn't react at all.

Georgette pasted one of her dim smiles on her face. How could she know that there was *something* to Yelena Essent if they didn't tell her? Georgette wasn't going to accept being stupid because she didn't know their—probably years and years old—gossip.

"Hmm," Laura said, kindly. "I suppose it is rather exotic sounding."

"Like the heroine of a novel."

"Or the villain," Carolyn countered. "I suppose you think in novels because your husband publishes them. I don't agree with novels and fiction myself. If you've time to read, why not read scriptures or Sunday school studies?"

Laura had clearly heard this riot before, but she simply sipped her tea and waited until Carolyn petered out.

Georgette simply didn't pick up the baton. There was no reason in wasting energy trying to convince a woman like Carolyn Holmes that fiction made the world more beautiful. That the moment when a book brought you to tears was a sort of witchcraft, a melding of spirits, of thoughts, ideas. That you could grow and learn and understand while reading *fiction* was something that had been shown time and again, but if you didn't have the wit to see it—well, tragic though it might be, you might just suffer from an incurable illness of the soul.

"Regardless," Carolyn said, as she realized that Georgette was smiling her simple smile again, "when Yelena Essent died, she died on a stormy night after suffering a quite unexpected illness. It is said that she died of a miscarriage."

Georgette winced and *just* kept herself from cupping where her baby must lie. This woman Carolyn was nearly preternatural in her ability to get under Georgette's skin.

"Or—" Carolyn drew out the word until Georgette almost demanded she get on with it. "Even an abortion."

The last word was whispered and Georgette's brows lifted.

"No one knows that," Laura said calmly. "It is an unfounded rumor and quite unkind. Yelena Essent died. Her husband mourned her terribly. That's all we can be sure of."

"Only because Dr. Fowler wouldn't have the wit to diagnosis it if Yelena was eight months gone and held

45

the dismantled corpse in her arms. That man needs to be run out of town chased by pitchforks and torches."

Georgette gagged and then said, "Oh dear, I must be going."

She hurried to pay her bill and heard Carolyn say, deliberately loud, "That woman is as dim as Polly Siegel."

Georgette closed her eyes against the rush of rage. She took in a deep breath and let it out slowly, making sure that breath was slow and easy. She repeated it as she paid and Mrs. Coach tittered uncomfortably. They could, after all, both hear Carolyn quite carefully.

"Being unwilling to gossip about the things you just said doesn't make her dim."

"That idiotic smile of hers does. She probably was married for money and that's how a *publisher* bought that huge old house. A publisher. I looked them up, you know. They published the book that caused those murders. There was an article about it recently. A woman writer wrote garbage and caused crime after crime. That's who should have been arrested. They were all the victims of her tripe nonsense."

"I like Mrs. Aaron. We've needed new blood in this town," Laura said, and the words chased Georgette from the tearoom. Really, Georgette thought, did Carolyn intend for Georgette to hear or was she just that obtuse about how her voice carried? The woman wouldn't be able to tell a secret in an empty forest to a tree without being overhead by half the village.

～

CHARLES AARON

"Robert," Charles said, after his nephew deposited a good half-dozen manuscripts on his desk. "I need you to find me a doctor."

"Are you all right?"

"Of course, I'm fine. The doctor in Harper's Hollow is an idiot. I need someone who will come to Harper's Hollow if needed." He cleared his throat and avoided Robert's avid gaze as he said, "Just in case. A—ah—precautionary measure."

"So you want a London doctor?" Robert was frowning at Charles and then his head tilted. "Georgette is expecting? Isn't it too soon to know?"

Charles scowled and Robert grinned widely.

"Don't ask," Robert nodded and made a note, "but find someone who works with ladies?"

Charles groaned and nodded.

"Who might be willing to make calls at odd hours?"

Charles sighed and said, "Don't tell anyone. I don't think I'm allowed until Georgette tells Eunice and Marian."

Robert considered and then said, "I just wanted to be sure I'm looking for the right thing, is all. I'll find a doctor who is quite well-respected, who works with ladies, and would be willing to come to you in Harper's Hollow for the event. Shall I start with neighboring towns?"

Charles nodded and then added, "If the nearest ones don't work, you might as well find someone in

London. While you're at it, find the name of a good agency for nannies."

Robert's grin grew even wider.

CHAPTER 6

GEORGETTE DOROTHY AARON

"*D*arling," Charles said as he lifted his briefcase to head out for the day. "I have a late dinner meeting with Mr. Pomeroy about his series of essays. Will you be all right?"

"Why wouldn't I be?" She patted his cheek. "Charles darling, I've had many a quiet evening by myself and honestly, it will be delightful to work without hammering of nails."

He kissed her nose and grinned at her. "You've had a surfeit of me, haven't you?"

"Maybe a little." She stepped back as he walked out the door, and she tugged his hand until he turned around, then she kissed his chin. "Maybe not."

He pressed another kiss to her nose and turned to leave again, but he paused. "Don't overdo."

Georgette just prevented herself from giving him a waspish reply. She slapped a smile on her face, but he knew her too well for that to work. His shout of laughter chased her back into the house. The men had already come and the clang of hammers echoed from the soon-to-be nursery. Her head was starting to pulse along with the sound of the pounding, and it would be a short while before she was holding a pillow over her head bemoaning a headache.

Instead of giving in to her fate, Georgette found her leather satchel with the long strap she liked to wear across her body. She loaded the bag with pencils and paper along with a sandwich, an apple, and a thermos of her favorite tea, loaded with cream and sugar. She'd rather drink it tepid than have anything else.

"Miss Georgie, are you escaping the racket?" Eunice's scowl told Georgette that Eunice was ready too.

Georgette nodded with unmasked glee. "Come along with me, dear Eunice. Bring your mending or a book and spend the afternoon by the river."

Eunice flinched at the sound of what must have been a sledgehammer. "Don't think I won't."

"Please do," Georgette said, starting to make a second sandwich. "I have missed you so, and I have much to speak to you about."

"We need a daily girl," Eunice told Georgette sourly, but she didn't object when Georgette added the second sandwich, apple, and two bottles of ginger beer to her satchel. "And a boy to help move all of that garbage out of the attics."

"Whatever you'd like," Georgette told Eunice. It was an edge of surreal shock that the answer was true. Georgette and Charles weren't rich, despite the size of their house, but they had enough for what was necessary and for many of their wants. What a blessing it was after struggling for so long. The biggest problem with being so blessed was feeling as though it wasn't quite right that she'd been given so much when others were continuing to struggle.

Eunice scowled. Her expression was vexed as she looked back at the house. "There is much to do."

"The racket might drive you mad and then who would take care of me?"

Eunice scoffed.

"Charles is dining in London. Let's just eat at the pub. Joseph said the beef stew was nearly as good as yours and it comes without the hammering."

Eunice didn't object. Instead she begrudgingly nodded.

Georgette and Eunice walked in silence as they left. They might technically be mistress and servant, but Eunice had half-raised Georgette, and each considered the other family.

"What do you think of Harper's Hollow?"

Eunice shrugged. "It's much the same to me. It wasn't as though either of us had bosom friends in Bard's Crook. The river is nice. The wood behind the house is nice."

"I'm almost positive I'm having a baby," Georgette said casually and Eunice stopped dead.

"A baby?" Her mouth pursed as she considered. "You've always been regular. If you're late, you've got a surprise inside."

"I'm late," Georgette said, bouncing on her toes a little. "I never thought I'd be saying that."

"A baby." Eunice's gaze widened. "I need white yarn and muslin and white ribbon. I don't like those attics rooms. They smell off and there's too much rustling. We need a cat immediately to rid ourselves of the vermin before the baby arrives."

"The room that has the wall being removed is the nursery," Georgette told Eunice. "Charles didn't like the original nursery either. He wants there to be more light."

"I always did like him."

Georgette laughed and then they spent the afternoon working. Her extra pencil and a few sheets of paper were claimed by Eunice who created a to-do list for the baby. It included things like a cradle, a baby blanket, and clothes.

"Are you going to hire a nanny?"

"What do you want?" Georgette's head tilted as she examined Eunice's face. "Do you want me to hire a housekeeper and cook instead? There is a part of me that wants to keep writing and a part of me that doesn't want to miss a second with the baby."

Eunice hesitated.

Georgette took a deep breath as the guilt hit her

again. "I'll need help. I don't want the same things as Marian. She wants to do everything, and—"

"You don't."

"I *like* being an author. I like how it makes me feel." Georgette hated how rotten she felt, as though she were letting her children down.

"I'm not telling you not to write, Miss Georgie." Eunice glanced at Georgette. "We were barely surviving when you started. Without that money, we'd have starved."

"I don't want to stop writing, but I don't want someone else to raise my baby."

"Darling," Eunice told her, taking Georgette's hand. "You write in the house. You can hire help, write, and go to your child whenever you want or they need you. I don't think I want to go back to the nursery either."

Georgette bit down on her bottom lip and confessed in a low voice, "I'm a little afraid to tell Charles I want a nanny."

Eunice laughed at Georgette, who scowled in return. "I bet you he hasn't even considered anything else."

Georgette shook off the thoughts, put her hand over her baby, and silently told the child, I'll love you more than I want to breathe, but Mommy wants to write too.

She turned back to the book she was writing. Scratching it out on the notebook paper was torture after having converted to a typewriter, and she wanted to stuff cotton in her ears and return to writing at home.

What if, she wondered, she wrote at Marian and Joseph's house? Oh! Georgette couldn't wait until Marian returned to the house on Friday to ask her. There was little concern, however, that Marian would object.

∼

EUNICE SMITH

After a while, Eunice stood and said, "I'm going to talk to the baker about likely fellows who might be interested in a job with us."

Georgette's mmmmed reply was unsurprising. Eunice would have been surprised if Georgette noticed she was gone. That girl had dove into books she was reading as hard as the ones she was writing. She was curled over the paper bundle, writing furiously.

Eunice found the grocer and started an order of the things they could use. As she did, she inquired about a gardener and a maid.

"You live at the old Essent place, yes?"

Eunice nodded. "It's a large house, as I'm sure you know. But there's just Mr. and Mrs. Aaron with an occasional friend or two."

The grocer's mouth twisted and he muttered, "You might have a bit of a time with that one."

Eunice frowned. "Mr. and Mrs. Aaron are kind to work for. They're hardly hard taskmasters."

"It's not that, it's the house."

Eunice lifted her brows. "They're fixing the house.

It's not like anyone expects a daily maid or a boy to scrub scratched floors into a shining."

The grocer paused and turned back from where he was filling her a bag of coffee. "No, no. It's not that. It's—"

Eunice waited.

"People think the house is haunted."

Eunice stared. She'd thought that the people who lived in Bard's Crook were idiots, but this man was winning. Haunted! Eunice had been living in it since the title transferred to Charles and Georgette. She had directed workmen, scrubbed the floors, hauled out garbage, and nothing had bothered her except the occasional mouse or spider.

"Nonsense."

"It's what people think."

"Pish-posh."

"You cannot pish-posh away superstitions."

Eunice frowned deeply. "Haunted?"

"Mr. Essent went mad when his wife died. Some say he killed her. A lot of that damage to the house was done by Mr. Essent after his wife died."

"So people won't take a good-paying job with kind people because the man who lived there before grieved his wife?" Eunice's cold judgement made the grocer flush. "Is this some kind of joke?"

"No, they think he murdered her."

She rocked back on her heels, arranged for the food to be delivered, and left before she could snap his ear off. She stalked to the baker, pushed through the door, scowled as she ordered a cake for Friday when

Joseph and Marian would return. Eunice's frown was fierce as she adjusted their breakfast buns order since Charles preferred toast with his breakfast, and Marian was going to stay through the next week. As she ordered, her ferocious frown didn't leave.

"Are you all right?" the baker asked.

"I just heard the most astonishing nonsense."

The baker lifted his brows and Eunice told him what the grocer said. The baker, however, didn't immediately leap in and contradict Eunice. "Do you really think that it's haunted?"

"No." Mr. Remington tapped the counter where he was placing cookies in a box. "What Mr. Devon didn't tell you was that Polly Siegel disappeared right around the same time that Yelena Essent died. Mr. Essent quite lost his mind. The house was in pristine condition only five years ago. It's like a bugbear in our little town, Eunice. The problem isn't just what happened to Mrs. Essent, who hadn't showed a trace of illness before she died. It's what happened to Polly Siegel. Because one of them is buried in the church yard and the other hasn't been seen in near five years."

Eunice wanted to shake the entirety of the town. There wasn't a better job than working for her Georgie and Mr. Charles. "Is there anyone desperate enough to work in the haunted house for good pay and kind masters or shall I start looking beyond Harper's Hollow?"

The baker's head tilted. "Are they offering room and board?"

Eunice paused. "They might. For the right situation."

"If your mistress wants to do a good deed as well, there's three kids who just lost their parents and don't have anywhere to go. The vicar is housing them right now, but—"

"How old are they?"

"I believe they're sixteen and seventeen. There's a fourteen-year-old as well."

Eunice had little doubt that they'd be welcome once Georgette heard of their tale.

Which she did as soon as she found Georgette still at her writing.

"There's no family?" Georgette had set aside her pencil and notebook to listen.

"I don't believe so," Eunice said.

"They must finish school. That's not negotiable. I won't take advantage of children to get some help with our dishes."

Eunice nodded. "They could go to school and come home and do the work together."

Georgette rose and stretched as she said, "Well let's go get them."

CHAPTER 7

GEORGETTE DOROTHY AARON

*E*unice and Georgette walked to the vicar's house through Harper's Hollow. It was in the main part of the town at the end of the street where the church held the place of honor. The church was grey bricks with a white steeple, and the vicarage, a plainer building, was immediately behind the church with the graveyard in between.

The three children were nearly grown, but not quite. The oldest child was one of two girls. She was hanging laundry. Though on the cusp of womanhood, she was dressed like a schoolgirl, her wheat-colored hair back in braids. Her face appeared and disappeared in between the movement of the clothes being pinned to the line. There were dark circles under her eyes and she nibbled her lip as she worked quickly. The look on her face was not one that had been provided comfort, and Georgette's heart ached at the sight.

She looked beaten, Georgette thought. It was more than grief. It was complete and utter dejection. Georgette pressed her hand to her heart as her gaze slowly moved to the boy. The next oldest, he was taller than both of the girls. His shoulders were narrow, showing his youth. He had dark circles under his eyes that matched both sisters along with the same pale hair. He worked as quickly and efficiently as his sister.

The youngest sat nearby. She was stick slim with long, pale hair braided back, red cheeks, and dark circles under her eyes highlighted by the shine of slow tears. She was snapping sugar peas. She, like the others, seemed utterly and completely broken.

"Hello," Georgette called. All three children's gazes snapped up. The boy and the younger girl turned back to their work without interest.

"Ma'am," the oldest girl said. "Can we help you?"

"I thought you might be able to," Georgette told them. "I'm looking for help at my house. I understand you need a place to stay."

The children glanced at each other and then back at Georgette. It was, she thought, the start to quite a spooky story, but Georgette intended them no ill will, and they weren't as spooked as they should be.

"All of us?" the oldest demanded with the dawning light of hope. "Even Janey?"

"Do you need a place to stay?" Georgette asked. "*All* of you?"

The boy nodded. "We do. Yes, ma'am. We'll do whatever it takes." He said the last with such pleading that Georgette understood at once.

"They are separating you?" Georgette demanded, pressing harder on her chest. "Why?"

"Janey is too young. She can go to an orphanage. She can finish school there. The vicar says it's best for her. Lucy and I are too old." The boy scratched the back of his neck. "She has the chance of a better future."

"Would you rather all stay in school and live with us?" Georgette offered, gesturing to Eunice. "I won't lie to you. We also need help."

The youngest squeaked but didn't speak. It was the oldest who replied this time. "We do."

"I have the room and a supposedly haunted house."

"What kind of help?" the boy asked, the haunted house part ignored in his desperation.

"In the kitchens, with the cooking, with the garden," Eunice said. "I'd expect you to help."

"And in exchange?" the boy asked.

"You'll have a home, food, and schooling. We could help each other."

"For *all* of us. Janey too?"

"Siblings are a blessing," Georgette told them. "I'm quite jealous of you, and yes, you can stay together."

"Where do you live?" the oldest girl asked.

"The old Essent place," Georgette said.

All three of them winced, glancing at each other

and weighing the offer. It seemed the superstition of the village had not escaped the three orphans.

"That's where Polly was last seen," the boy replied. "She was my friend."

"I don't know about Polly," Georgette told him. "I just know that no one wants the job because of whatever happened there before. It's why your names came up."

"It is," the oldest girl added. "I'm Lucy, this is Eddie, and our sister, Janey. We want to stay together. You just want help around your house? Like chores? That's it?"

Georgette and Eunice glanced at each other, looked back at the children, and nodded.

"*And* we can go to school?" Eddie demanded. Like schooling was a gift.

"Do you want to go to school?"

"I want to be a doctor," Eddie told her. His fists clenched as he prepared for a scoffing reaction.

"That's a high goal," Georgette told him. "You'll have to study hard. You'll need a tutor. Charles will know about that."

Eddie stared and Lucy moved, pulling Janey to her feet. "We're going to do this."

They went to speak to the vicar's wife, Mrs. Oddington, and she looked so relieved, Georgette whispered to Eunice that they might have made a terrible mistake.

Only, Mrs. Oddington was making cabbage soup for supper. They couldn't afford the children, Georgette realized. They were, perhaps, taking food from their children's mouths to feed the orphans. Mrs. Oddington tried to ask the right questions, but she also added some preserved meat to the soup. Their dinner just got better when she realized she wouldn't have to feed three more.

"You can look after them from a distance," Georgette told the vicar's wife. "We aren't far, and I'm sure it'll be good for them to know others care."

The final shreds of guilt faded from Mrs. Oddington's eyes and she nodded, kissing each child and helping them to gather their things. "You do have so much room."

"We do," Georgette agreed. "It helps all of us."

They left soon after.

"It occurs to me," Georgette said as the house came into view, "that I might have discussed this with Charles first."

Eunice snorted evilly. "I wondered when it would."

"You could have said something."

The children gave each other concerned looks with the littlest tearing up.

"Don't worry," Georgette said. "He won't object. Just do well in school, be quiet around his office, and work reasonably hard. Charles is kinder than I am."

"Only to you," Eunice told Georgette. "He loves you."

The children started again.

Eunice sighed. "He's a kind man. Don't worry. He won't turn you away."

"We will work hard," Eddie swore. "We will do whatever you need. They were going to send Janey to an orphanage. Me and Lucy were going to have to get jobs, and I'd have never been a doctor. My mama would have said that you were an answer to prayers."

GEORGETTE'S HANDS were on her hips as she stared into the first of the two servants' attic rooms. The storage had overflowed into the nursery with, as Eunice had declared, too much scuttling for anyone's comfort. Both rooms were of an equal size and both had metal frames and thin mattresses that had been mouse homes.

"We need cats," Georgette said. "Immediately."

Janey gasped. "We had a cat! I could get her! She was a good mouser!"

"Well, of course," Georgette said and Janey was running down the stairs before anyone else could say a word.

Lucy's laugh of joy was echoed by Eddie.

"I don't know if one cat will be enough."

"There's a woman who lived near us with kittens," Lucy said. "Their mama was a good mouser. The kittens probably are."

Georgette's dogs were snuffling and Georgette's head tilted. Three dogs...three cats? "Ask Eunice how many to get."

"She has a pair of rather attached ones," Lucy said carefully. Her gaze was afraid to hope, but Georgette guessed Lucy had become attached to those kittens.

Georgette smiled. "Lucy love, get whichever ones

you think best. A pair of kittens who adore each other is fine with me."

When Lucy left to find Eunice, Georgette turned to Eddie, who was eying her carefully. "This feels too good to be true."

"You seem like good children to me. Maybe being able to keep your cat is the answer to your mother's prayer, like you said."

Eddie swallowed thickly, his Adam's apple bobbing. "We tried to be good. You only want us to help around the house?" He was so suspicious, so... concerned she wanted something more that Georgette wondered if Lucy or Janey had been inappropriately propositioned.

"Eddie," Georgette examined his face, the dark circles under his eyes. He and Lucy had been sleepless as they'd tried to decide what to do after losing both of their parents. "I understand what it's like to be you."

"How can you?" he demanded. His accusing gaze on the oversized house was disbelieving.

"I wasn't that much older than Lucy when my parents died, but I had Eunice. I know the hurt of that, however. It's not fair you lost your house, and your cat, and were losing each other. All we can do is take the chances we're given, work hard to craft the life we want, and trust that not all of mankind is out to take advantage of us."

Eddie frowned at Georgette, but he nodded.

"Do you have a final year left of school?"

He nodded.

"I expect you to study hard for the exams for

university. We'll try for a scholarship and if that doesn't happen, we'll see what we can do."

His jaw dropped, and she patted his arm.

"How were you going to go to school before your parents died?"

"I'd learned about a scholarship, and I hoped to find work. The vicar was studying with me to help me prepare."

Georgette nodded and then said, "You'll need to scrub these rooms down and throw out the furniture. We are making quite an unsightly heap in the back garden while we get rid of all the skeletons of broken furniture. We'll get some better beds, but until then, cots are all we have."

The boy nodded as Georgette made a list for him and his sisters. It wasn't much, and it was all for their bedroom. They'd paint later, and they'd fix that cracked window later. One of the rooms would be for the girls, one for Eddie. They'd be all right. Now to explain to Charles.

The afternoon ended as the workmen left. One of them helped Eddie carry the old bed frames out to the garden and agreed to take them away. The bare pads that could hardly be called mattresses were going to be burned in the garden. While Eddie and Janey scrubbed down the empty rooms, Lucy met Eunice in the kitchen to help get the stew and berry pie from the pub.

Once they'd eaten, Georgette returned to her new story of Harper's Bend. It was easier to write now that the actual lives of characters that she'd based off of villagers had stopped infecting her story.

The doctor who had once been Dr. Wilkes was just Dr. Williams now. He was his own creature, and he almost told his own story as the antics of his demon children charmed Georgette on the pages. She had given the doctor and his wife a soon-to-arrive baby.

As she wrote, she realized that even though she had never lived anywhere else, she did not miss Bard's Crook. In fact, the only thing she missed was her little house, but this bigger, more beautiful house was quickly replacing that small cottage in her mind as home.

A young couple had purchased the cottage while she and Charles had been traveling, and there would soon be small feet pattering around the floors where Georgette and her mother had once learned to walk. Georgette would have regretted the same being lost for her child, but this house—this house called to her spirit.

It was a bit like Marian had said. The old Georgette fit the cottage where she had been raised. The new Georgette fit this big old house with its layers upon layers of stories. She didn't want her child to be the overlooked wallflower or the town's personal cipher. She didn't want him or her to grow up defined before the first breath had been taken.

CHAPTER 8

The goddess Atë had not expected Georgette to take on the orphans. She wasn't surprised that Georgette had. It was possible that no one knew Georgette Dorothy Aaron better than the goddess Atë. It was just that the children would bring out in Georgette responsibility and carefulness far more than anything else could, which would really destroy Atë's viewing pleasure.

Atë considered turning her eye to the village in the north with the funny little man who had discovered a recent crime, but Georgette was delightful. Like a kitten chasing a light. Atë watched as Georgette left her house with its secrets and walked towards the train station. The last train was coming in for the night, and she'd been writing for so long that her back ached.

She wandered slowly towards the train station and

found that it had been early for once and Charles was
already walking towards her in the dimming light.

"Georgette?"

She slipped her arm through his and pressed a kiss
to his cheek. "There you are."

"Did you miss me after all?"

"No," Georgette said instantly and then laughed at
the look on his face. "I'm afraid I didn't think about
you nearly as much as I should have. I confess I was
distracted."

Charles paused and looked down at her. "Is this
where you tell me you took a lover?"

She grinned at the look on his face and shook her
head.

"Is this where you tell me that you burned the
house down?"

She shook her head.

"Is this where I discover that you've bought a
steamship ticket to Nice?"

Georgette laughed.

"What then?"

"It all started with discussing a nanny with Eunice."

Georgette paused for Charles to object. To tell her
it was her duty, but he just nodded and said, "Robert
figured out you are expecting but is prepared to be
silent and surprised at the appropriate moment. He is
finding a good service for us to find an excellent
nanny. Along with a doctor who isn't a fool."

All those worries Georgette had possessed about a
nanny and for no reason. He had already started
thinking of it. "You don't think it should be me?"

"Nannying?" Charles frowned. "I think you should write."

"Even though we'll have a child?"

"That's what nannies are for, Georgette. You're a very good writer, and it's not like you won't be there if our baby needs you."

She'd had scolded herself for being worried over nothing, but they were getting closer to the house and Charles still didn't know about the teenage orphans.

"So, after we talked about the nanny, Eunice said we needed a daily maid."

Charles just nodded. "We do. Eunice isn't as young as she could be. The house is too much even for a young woman."

"She's not *old*," Georgette hissed. Eunice was in her late 40s, and she was going to live forever.

Charles wrapped his arm around Georgette. "All I'm saying, darling, is that someone else can scrub the floors."

"Yes, well. No one wants to work for us. Our house is haunted, apparently. The wife of the previous owner died rather unexpectedly. Rumors abound! Supposedly the master bedroom was perfect five years ago, Mrs. Essent died, and Mr. Essent grieved by destroying their bedroom."

Charles's head tilted and he said, "It's ridiculous, but I can just imagine it given the state of the room."

"Then the baker told Eunice about some young people who might be willing to work for us. Since they were desperate."

Charles shook his head. "It would seem that a paying job would be reason enough to work for us."

"Well," Georgette added, rushing now. "I met them. They're orphans, Charles, and they want to go to school, especially the boy. He wants to be a doctor. They're good kids, and they were being separated, and the next thing I knew I was telling them they could have a bedroom and live with us, but they'd have to do the work of the daily maid, study hard, and be quiet around your office and then I thought, 'Oh no. You haven't talked to Charles about it.' But they were going to be separated, and we're locked in now because the guilt will destroy me if we separate them."

Charles stopped walking at Georgette's frantic rushed confession. "So you found us help. Children who are old enough but who are orphaned."

Georgette nodded.

"And you expect me to be upset that you took in needy children in our oversized house?"

Georgette bit down on her lip and guessed, "No?"

"No." He pressed a kiss against her forehead. "If they're good kids and they want to study *and* they'll help Eunice? I'm sold on the idea."

Georgette sighed in relief. "I was so worried."

"I'm working from home tomorrow," Charles said.

Georgette had to wonder if he had changed his plans because of her, but she didn't ask. If he was being protective, she wasn't going to tease him about it. They stopped in the shadow of the willow tree to kiss and then found their way inside the house. The children had worked hard over the course of the day, moving their things, cleaning their rooms, making up their cots until better beds could be located.

"Oh," Georgette told him as they opened the door. "We have cats now. Mostly because of the mice in the attics."

"Do they have names?"

"Well the children had a cat who had been left at the house when they were taken in. They went and rescued her and her name is Biscuit."

"I approve," Charles told Georgette. "And the others?"

"They're unnamed at the moment. We ended up with the last three kittens from some person Lucy knew. They were to be drowned on Monday if they were not taken by someone, so Lucy took them all and then said she'd return one if she had to."

"We'll keep the poor mite," Charles agreed. "You know before I met you I was a childless, petless, bachelor who spent the evening smoking and reading."

"You can still smoke and read." Georgette told him. "Only now you'll have to pet a cat while you do."

∼

GEORGETTE DOROTHY AARON

On Friday morning with a drizzle in the air that would prevent a writing session by the river, Georgette told the children, "Let's see if we can find beds for you in the attics."

The children glanced up from their breakfast of

porridge and toast and then agreed. They had been extremely respectful and hard working for Eunice over the past days. Georgette might have been worried, but she'd been visited by several people who had known the children and said they'd always been respectful and hard working. The flu had taken their parents and a little sister, and they'd been left alone.

A tragedy certainly. They were good children who had been well-raised long before Georgette and Eunice had stuck their oar in. It had been three days since Charles had met the children, and he liked them as much as Georgette and Eunice did. The relief was nearly overwhelming to Georgette.

"Eddie," Charles said, "you help bring boxes down. I know that Georgette wants to sort and throw away the waste of ages. As soon as the heavy work is done, though, you'll need to turn to your studies. Being a doctor and getting a scholarship is going to require hours daily. At least five before school starts."

The boy's gaze widened with hope again. Perhaps he'd wondered in the last few days that they'd only offered to get him to work. It had been three days since Charles had met the children, and he liked them. The relief was nearly overwhelming to Georgette.

"What about you, Lucy?" Charles asked. "What do you want?

"I always wanted to just be like my mom," Lucy said quietly. "To marry and have a family."

"And you've completely your schooling?"

She nodded.

Charles's head tilted. "Well, you're welcome to stay

with us until that happens or you shift your dreams. School can happen for girls, too. I'm sure we can find one for you if you decide what you want to learn."

She nodded silently. His gaze dropped to Janey, who ate with their old cat on her lap. The youngest of them was nearly always silent, and Charles just looked at her for a moment and then returned to the paper.

They finished breakfast in silence and then Georgette took the children up to the attics with her. They were dark, not because there were no windows, but because the windows were grimy. Georgette frowned fiercely as Eunice and Eddie appeared with buckets.

"The windows first, I think."

Eunice nodded and took Janey with her to scrub the windows while Georgette stared farther into the attics. The servants' bedrooms were easily accessible by the servant stairs and they'd been left mostly untouched. The nursery, however, had been crowded with what looked like decades of anything and everything.

Georgette pointed to the corner where a full-sized bed was standing. If it was functional, they could get a mattress. In front of the bed, however, was a dresser, trunk, and boxes upon boxes of nonsense. Georgette and Eddie moved the boxes down to the floor below and then pulled the bed out. It had quite a colony of mice living in it, given the renewed scuttling, and Georgette might have jumped and darted back before rubbing her arms briskly and helping Eddie to move the bed.

"This will work for Lucy and Janey," Georgette

said, "if they shared. Let's just get those fellows to carry the bed to the room for us, and Lucy can scrub it down. Eddie, take the mattress to be burned and send the fellows in."

Georgette watched as the bed was carried out. Behind it was another bed tilted on its side. It was smaller and just might do for Eddie's bedroom. They couldn't continue with cots for the children. Not with their hard work and their studies. They needed to sleep well at night.

"Lucy, dear," Georgette said, "would you help me tip this down?"

Together the two of them worked and got the bed from its side to the floor. It was a solid bed, Georgette thought. They just needed another mattress. She wiped her brow, sneezed, and then said, "Have the men come take this one to Eddie's room, would you?"

Lucy hurried out, and Georgette frowned at the nursery. How much of it was filled with perfectly functional beds like this one? She started to circle the bed and noted a pile of clothes just tossed behind it. Really, Georgette thought, how hard would it have been to put those clothes in a trunk? Then she saw the shoes and she frowned. What an odd way to toss the clothes with shoes, almost as if they'd laid out an outfit for the day on the ground of the attic.

And then, tilted a bed over it? The frown became almost painfully deeper. Finally she saw what her mind had been trying to register. In the darkest corner of the nursery, behind two beds, a dresser, and a series of boxes and trunks, was the remains of what had been a person—a very small person.

"Oh dear heavens," Georgette gasped. The workmen came in with Lucy, and Georgette stared blankly at them.

"Ma'am?"

Georgette snapped, "Out. Everyone out. Right now."

They looked at her like she was mad, but Eunice knew Georgette well enough to identify distress. The woman snaked her hand around Janey's wrist, and then hissed to the men, "You heard her. We'll have you move it later."

Georgette shooed everyone out of the attics and locked the door behind her.

"Georgie?" Eunice asked carefully. She'd sent Janey on ahead down the stairs and the workmen back to their tasks before she'd asked the question. Georgette dared to slip down to her bottom on the steps.

"Take the children in the kitchen and keep them with you. Send Charles up. Have the children *scrub* up, and—" She placed her head between her knees and moaned, "Oh God, Eunice. There was a skeleton in there. Behind that bed. It was smaller than Janey. There is the skeleton of a child in that attic."

"Are you sure?" Eunice demanded, aghast.

Georgette nodded against her knees. "Say nothing to the children."

"Of course." Eunice pressed her hand against Georgette's hair. "It will be okay, Miss Georgie."

"For us perhaps," Georgette muttered into her

knees. "That little girl won't be okay. She hasn't been all right for some time."

Eunice didn't answer. She headed down the stairs, but Charles came running a few minutes later. "She said it was an emergency."

"Did she tell you?" Georgette lifted her head finally.

"Are you all right? Is it the baby?"

"No," Georgette said. "Charles—" She shook her head and then pressed her fingers to her temples to hold in the fierce pounding. "There's a dead child in the attic."

He blinked and then slowly frowned. "I'm sorry, what?"

"There's a dead child in the attic. Given the dress, it's a girl."

"You can't tell?"

"The poor thing has been there for a while, Charles. All that is left is a skeleton, hair, and clothes. There's a dead little girl in *our attic.*"

Charles took a seat next to Georgette and asked again. "Are you sure?"

Georgette's answer was to curl sideways onto his lap and take shaky, shaky breaths in. She moaned a little, feeling sick. Was it the baby making her feel sick? Or was it the body? Georgette had no idea, but she didn't want to move.

"Georgette, we need to call someone. We need to do something."

"We don't have a telephone yet," Georgette said weakly. "We don't have...oh my goodness, Charles. Someone else's baby is dead in our attic. It has to be the girl, Polly Siegel. I thought our neighbors were fools to associate a missing girl with our house. She didn't even live here, but they were right."

"Georgette," Charles said. "Give me the key to the attic."

She handed it over him and then she put her head back between her knees while he opened the door. She could hear the click of his shoes on the floor of the attic. He paused and stood for too long. Perhaps his mind also stuttered over the sight. Georgette couldn't help but imagine it again, and she had to take long, slow breaths to stay calm until he returned.

"We need to get help."

Georgette nodded into her knees and slowly rose as Charles locked the door once again. She swayed, making him gasp and grab her arm. Charles lifted her into his arms and carried her down to the first floor. Once there, he said, "We have to call for help."

She was shaking as she replied. "I'm all right. It just hit me all at once. There's a house a ways down." She pointed to the left, and they rushed towards it together. Hand-in-hand, somehow the horror seemed a little lessened.

CHAPTER 9

CHARLES AARON

*G*eorgette had held a woman's hand while she suffered from a poisoning that might well have killed her. While Georgette watched, she hadn't faltered. Georgette had once watched a man level a gun at the auto that contained the supposed author Joseph Jones. Georgette hadn't faltered, swayed, or weakened. He'd carried her home that time, but it had been for his comfort rather than hers.

She hadn't swayed when she'd faced off with the man who had been intent on murdering Aunt Parker for turning down his marriage proposal. She hadn't swayed when she'd left her home behind or when she'd sold him her first book, terrified and hungry.

That she had swayed today scared Charles more

than he could have guessed was possible. A part of him wanted to tuck her into bed, but he also had no intentions of letting her out of his sight. He wanted to know she was well because his eyes were on her, ready to catch her, help her, or comfort her.

There was something horrible about being in love, Charles thought, as he squeezed her hand a little tighter and hurried towards the red brick house that was set back from the street. There was something horrible about loving someone so much and realizing that if they were taken from you—like the little girl had been taken from her family—that you'd never stop missing them.

If Charles lost Georgette now, he could return to his rooms in London. He could return to eating at the club, and he could return to dinners and plays with elegant women, but he'd never be all right again. The joy of *Midsummer's Night Dream* would be gone for him now that he'd seen it with Georgette. The comfort of sleeping in his bed would be over now that he'd curled his body around hers. He wasn't sure he'd even be able to drink tea again. Just thinking about this was making him ill.

They opened the gate and Charles led the way up to the door where he knocked sharply. A woman with a wrinkled face and kind eyes opened the door, wiping her hands on her apron. "Hello."

"Ma'am," Charles said, nodding once. "Do you have a telephone?"

The woman nodded and then Charles said, "There's an emergency. We need to use it."

She stepped back, and Charles pulled Georgette with him. "We'll pay," Georgette told the woman, even though she had raised no objections.

"Is there anything I can do?" The woman's gaze was moving between Georgette and Charles. "Are you all right, my dear? You're quite white and well—dusty."

It was Charles who answered. "She could use a cup of tea. Heavy on the milk and sugar."

"Well, who couldn't use just that when there's been a shock?" The woman disappeared and came back quickly with a cup of tea. It was dark and strong and smelled of cinnamon and orange. "It's my favorite, but it's a bit odd. It's ready now, however."

Georgette took a sip and then oohed.

The woman smiled at Georgette and then said, "I'm Anna Mustly."

"Georgette Mar—oh, Aaron." She grinned and said, "It's a new name."

"Newlyweds?"

Georgette nodded, smiling as she always did when her wedding was discussed. Then Charles started to speak and the joy fled.

As Charles explained what they had found over the telephone, Anna Mustly gasped and took a seat. She seemed as shaky as Georgette. "Oh no. It must be Polly. Was she quite small?"

"She seemed like a child," Georgette said, sipping the tea again as she shivered against a sudden chill. "Like a little girl."

Mrs. Mustly took Georgette's hand as if she needed the comfort too.

"Oh child. Oh child. Oh child. We did love her so."
Tears fell down her cheeks. "We knew, of course. But
we hoped. It was nice to have hope."

Georgette sipped her tea with a trembling hand
while Mrs. Mustly dug out a handkerchief. They heard
Charles adjust the call to Scotland Yard and Mrs.
Mustly gasped. "Scotland Yard?"

"He's calling his nephew," Georgette told her. "He
was coming anyway, but if he can come sooner, it
would be nice to have the support. It's so awful."

She found a tear had rolled down her own cheek as
she looked at Mrs. Mustly. The woman hadn't stopped
crying and was dabbing her tears as she gently rocked
back and forth.

"She was like a gift straight from heaven. I know
many people wouldn't see it. But I did. My poor
Barnaby did. Her mother and brothers did. A child like
that—you'd think that she'd be a burden, but she
wasn't. Her mother said every day with Polly was a
joy. Her brothers had all offered to take the girl when
her mother couldn't care for her anymore. She wasn't
like us, you see. She was a little simple. A song in her
heart, light in her eyes, but she didn't understand the
world around her. To her, everything was beautiful."

Georgette pressed her fingers to her mouth as she
heard Charles explaining to Joseph. She didn't catch so
much the words as the feel of the back and forth. She
felt Charles's gaze on her and wished she could stop
crying, but she couldn't. It was too much to find someone's special angel in her attic.

"Was she sick?" Georgette asked.

"Oh no." Mrs. Mustly shook her head and dabbed her tears again. "Not Polly. Healthy as an ox. We spent the day with her, Barnaby and I did. We had a picnic. We baked. It was a lovely day, and she was in good health."

"Is her being missing why people think the house is haunted?"

Mrs. Mustly's laugh was dark. "No, dear. No. Being haunted by sweet Polly would be a gift. Nothing to do with our girl. We all thought she wandered off and got lost. Maybe got hurt and couldn't get home. She did like to wander, but we all looked after her, didn't we? We knew she was special. We'd take her by the hand and bring her home. We'd invite her to pick apples or berries and then bring her home to her mama. I suppose we thought she'd suffered an accident. We looked for her, we did. We looked for her for weeks and weeks. We looked for her long after we knew she wasn't coming home."

Georgette's hands were still shaking as Charles told her, "We need to get back to the house for the constables."

Georgette slowly rose and then hugged Mrs. Mustly tightly. The woman welcomed the hug and squeezed Georgette nearly as hard. "I'm sorry."

Mrs. Mustly sniffed and then said, "I'm the one who's sorry. I should have come over and greeted you. I should have told you that you were welcome. I just mixed your house with Yelena Essent in my mind. I hate to admit I despised her."

"It's all right," Georgette said, squeezing her tightly.

"Thank you for finding our Polly."

Georgette shuddered, nodded, and let Charles pull her with him back to the house. The constables arrived with an ambulance as they walked into the house. Eunice and the children came out when Georgette and Charles arrived, but Eunice kept them to the side of the garden, unable to hear.

Charles handed over the key and the constable went inside with him. They came back in mere minutes and Georgette was questioned. She described what they'd done. Moving furniture and boxes to get to the beds. It was only when Lucy and Georgette had righted the second bed that Georgette had been able to find the body hidden behind all of the mess.

It was only as she said it that Georgette thought: hiding the body. Hiding the body. Hiding the body. There was no way that a healthy little girl had crawled into that particular spot and died. No, Georgette thought. Polly Siegel had been *put* there. She must have been. She had been put there and then the furniture had been placed over her, the boxes had been placed in front of her. They'd layered her in and left her. If Mr. Essent hadn't sold the house, Polly Siegel would have gone undiscovered for who knew how long.

Long enough for her killer to pretend he hadn't done what he'd done. Long enough for her mother to move away from the memories. Long enough for her little body to turn to bones and dust. Long enough for someone to think they'd gotten away with something horrible. Long enough for Georgette and Charles to be drawn to the house.

Why were they so cursed? Georgette wondered. But then she thought of Anna Mustly who had cried with an edge of relief. Those who loved her and known Polly wasn't coming back. They'd looked and looked and looked and now the question of what had happened to her was solved. She could be buried with her kin and they would be able to start finding answers.

Maybe, Georgette thought, she'd been pulled to that house by a ghost. But it hadn't been a ghost with ill intent. It hadn't been a vengeful spirit. It had been a little girl who wanted her mother to stop crying over what had happened to her and stop wondering if she should have done something differently. Maybe a little girl who just wanted her mother and brothers and friends to know she had died and that it was all right if they let go of her.

CHAPTER 10

JOSEPH AARON

"You've got a call sir," one of the boys said.

Joseph nodded and told them to send it through. His mind was on the series of robberies that had been hitting businesses near the dock, and it took him a minute to snap to the matter at hand even when his extension rang.

"Joseph?" Charles's tinny voice was immediately identifiable, as was the stress in his uncle's voice.

"Charles?"

"My god, Joseph, there's a body in our attic!"

"A what?"

"Georgette says it's a little girl. A skeleton. It was behind furniture."

"Hidden?"

"Yes, I think, yes. Georgette looked as if she was about to stumble down the stairs and there was nothing I could for the child. Long dead, it seems. They're saying it's—" His voice turned from the phone and he asked, "Are you certain?"

The question wasn't directed to Joseph and Charles asked a follow up question and then said, "The neighbor believes it must be a missing girl, Polly Siegel."

"Like my house?" Joseph demanded, suddenly feeling sick. "Is that why the woman moved away? Her daughter had disappeared?"

"Yes. She's been missing for nearly five years. Who else could it be?"

Joseph muttered a curse. "I'll call the local boys if I can—"

Another of the young officers stuck his head into Joseph's office. "Sir, the chief inspector wants to see you."

"Charles, I've got to go. I'll call the local constables as soon as I can. You notified them?"

"Yes, yes, of course. It was my first call. Joseph, we could use you, if it's possible. I—I'm worried about Georgette."

Joseph frowned deeply and thought there was something more in his uncle's voice. Georgette was a bundle full of sweet trouble. When you combined Georgette with Joseph's own Marian, there was little doubt that he and his uncle would be chasing after their ladies, scattered and worried for the rest of their lives.

"I'll do what I can," Joseph said again. He hung up on his uncle and hurried to his supervisor's office.

"Sir?" Joseph asked.

"We've an odd case, Aaron. You've been asked for. Seems a little girl was found in that town you bought a house in. The locals there want you assigned."

"I just heard," Joseph said, dropping into the seat across from his supervisor. "My uncle called me. His wife found the body."

"Yes, well, I don't envy you this one. The ones that include children always turn my stomach and haunt me for years after. Could be an accident, we'll see. Either way, the mother is living in London now." He shoved a paper towards Joseph. "You'll have to tell her that her little girl has been found."

Joseph's stomach dropped. Nothing was worse. He'd decided to work for Scotland Yard after getting his own knock at the door when he was a boy. There had been an accident. His parents had died. It had taken Charles a few hours to get to Joseph and Robert, and the constable had stayed with them, holding Robert's hand while Joseph had curled in on himself. Now Joseph was going to have to do something similar. There was nothing worse.

He sighed and took the address. All that he looked forward to that morning faded away. "I'll give your robbery case to Stebbins," his supervisor said. "Fill him in and go."

Joseph nodded and left, pulling one of the new constables with him. He wrote a quick note to Marian and sent it off. He had little doubt Marian and her dog would be on the next train to Harper's Hollow. If he'd had his druthers, Marian would stay home, but Joseph didn't need her to tell him that she was going to Georgette's side. At least Charles was there and Joseph was on his way. Marian would be safe enough.

CORNELIA SIEGEL LIVED in a row house near a little park. There were flowers hanging from the front porch, and they also lined the walk. It looked as though there was a shared garden behind the house, and despite the fact that she had a missing daughter, the house seemed happy. If a house could seem happy, that was. Joseph supposed he was being fanciful because he did not want to go up that walk, use the lion knocker, and then remove the last shreds of hope that Mrs. Siegel felt.

He sighed deeply and opened the gate. There was a twitch at the window curtain, but he didn't look towards it. He proceeded with a count in his head, so he wasn't dragging his feet. An odd feeling to be sure. His assistant, Constable Rogers, was just behind him and they would know by the sight of his uniform that something was amiss.

"Keep quiet, pay attention. I'll need your help with the details after the fact."

"Yes, sir."

The door opened just before Joseph could knock. On the other side of it was a woman who must have been nearing sixty years old. She had gray hair pulled back from her face in a bun, her eyes were blue and they were already starting to tear.

"Is it Polly?"

Joseph nodded.

"They found her finally?"

Joseph cleared his throat and attempted to control his sympathy. He took a deep breath and said gently, "May we come in?"

Mrs. Siegel stepped back. There was the sound of children in the garden and someone was in the kitchens given the noise of pots. She cleared her throat, glanced towards the kitchen, and paused. But then she took the seat, waving them to sit as well.

Joseph took the seat next to her, but at an angle, so he could see her face, leaving the seat across the way for Rogers to sit in observation.

"Please tell me."

"There was the body of a child found in Harper's Hollow. The immediate assumption is that it is your daughter, but the local constables are still recovering her. Identification will be...difficult."

"She wore a locket," Mrs. Siegel said. "Did anyone see a locket?"

"I don't know the details yet, Mrs. Siegel. I'll be leaving here and going there soon. You don't seem surprised that she was found, Mrs. Siegel."

"I'm not," she said, wiping a tear away. "My Polly would have come home to me if she could have. I've known since the early days she was gone."

"I hope you'll allow me to convey my deepest

condolences," Joseph said carefully. "I'll do all I can find to find out what happened to your daughter."

"She was murdered," Mrs. Siegel told Joseph flatly. "She was a bit simple, you know? She was simple, she was sweet, she was kind. An angel. If it weren't murder, we'd have found her a long time ago. Where was she found?"

Joseph considered for a moment, but he wanted this unfettered reaction. "She was found in the Essent attic. It was sold recently. The new couple has been doing construction and cleaning out the decades of garbage, and they found her."

Mrs. Siegel closed her eyes and nodded. She seemed entirely unsurprised. "Yelena didn't help search for Polly. Yelena must have known. She claimed to be too ill to come to the funeral, but—"

Mrs. Siegel's mouth snapped shut and she wiped another tear. "It seems God has saved me from murder as well. At least for Yelena."

"What do you mean?" Joseph asked.

"Where was my Polly? The attic or the cellars?"

"The attic," Joseph said carefully, watching as the mother thought. She seemed to form conclusions and abandon them one after another. "How did you know?"

"Where else would have hidden the smell? They just had one woman who helped them. Her senses weren't what they could have been, something about an accident. I always thought Yelena preferred her servant half-blind, half-dead, and uncaring to hide what she was up to."

"Ah," Joseph said. "I see."

Mrs. Siegel's words were vicious and Joseph would have doubted them except the body *had* been found.

"The servant, Morry, never used the cellars or the attic. She had a hard time getting around and flat out refused to go either place. If they were clever about how they hid my Polly, or if they'd done anything to help hide the smell, Morry almost certainly would have missed it."

"Do you really believe it was deliberate? Do you think this woman killed your daughter?"

Mrs. Siegel paused then and Joseph waited, knowing regardless of the validity of her argument, it might provide light on what *actually* happened.

"Yelena Essent was many things. She was spoilt, difficult, beautiful, and she was nearly helpless. Polly was small, but she would have been too heavy for someone like Yelena to move. Especially as a dead weight. I couldn't have lifted my Polly and carried her up flights of stairs, and Yelena had only Morry who would not have helped. Morry would have told the constables and watched without reaction as her mistress got dragged off to prison."

"What if this Yelena somehow tricked Polly into the attic?"

"Polly didn't like Yelena. She wouldn't have gone up to the attic with her. She wouldn't have crossed the garden to Yelena."

"Not even for sweets or to see a kitten or a doll?"

Mrs. Siegel paused for a long time and then shook

her head. "Polly *really* didn't like Yelena. I don't think Polly would have gone."

"What if she were ordered?"

"If someone yelled at Polly, she'd have gone running for me or one of the other people she trusted. She was terrified of shouting. You have to understand, she wasn't like a regular child. She was nearly full-grown for a normal child, but she wasn't. She couldn't read. She still played with dolls. She didn't understand most social interactions."

"Wouldn't that make her more likely to be tricked?"

Mrs. Siegel shook her head again. "Polly was harder to persuade. Her reactions were generally kind and sweet, but you couldn't talk her into liking someone she didn't like. You couldn't get her to stay with you if you were shouting, she'd run and hide. No, no. Polly wouldn't have gone with Yelena. Polly wouldn't have been ordered up there, and a fighting Polly? A hundred times harder to move than her sleeping. Or...or...dead. No."

Joseph considered. As much as he wanted to chalk up this idea to hysteria or a personal grievance for Mrs. Essent, it was well-reasoned.

"So you believe she was taken there after she died?" Joseph asked and watched Mrs. Siegel nod without hesitation.

The woman seemed utterly convinced, and Joseph didn't have any reason to doubt her yet. He filed the information away, not wanting to take notes.

"Polly was simple. She didn't bother with manners. If Yelena had asked my Polly to come with her somewhere, Polly would have laughed and run off. Polly spent a fair amount of time on that side of the wood, but it was because she loved Mr. and Mrs. Mustly. It had nothing to do with Yelena Essent." Mrs. Siegel said the name like it was an insult.

"Where is Yelena now?" Joseph asked.

"She's dead, and good riddance to her. I hope she's enjoying a long stay in hell."

Joseph shifted, but didn't argue with her. He certainly didn't blame a mother for feeling that way about the woman she assumed killed or hid the death of a child. In truth, if Yelena Essent were responsible, Joseph hoped she was burning as well.

"What happened to Yelena?"

"Oh a month or two after Polly went missing, she supposedly got sick."

"Supposedly?"

"Rumors were flying she was with child and suffered a miscarriage. The meaner of us assumed she had an abortion and it went sideways."

Joseph blinked rather rapidly, holding in a reaction. Miscarriage? Abortion?

"Why would she need to hide a child? She was married, wasn't she?"

"Her husband wasn't able to have children. It was a side effect of the war or an illness. I never knew the details. If she *was* with child, it was proof that the spoiled, whining wife he'd indulged endlessly was cuckolding him."

Joseph winced and then asked, "What about Mr.

Essent? Do you think he was involved in what happened to Polly?"

"I don't know," Mrs. Siegel said. "He traveled a lot. He could have easily been gone when Polly disappeared. I think perhaps he was? I don't know. *I don't know.* She must have been so scared." The tears started then, and Joseph took her arm. She leaned into him, and he wrapped his arm around her. She cried and Joseph held her hand, thinking of when he'd had his own visit from the constables.

There was a sound in the hallway, and Joseph looked up to see someone closer to his age. The woman was wearing an apron and staring in utter shock at Mrs. Siegel almost in Joseph's arms.

"Mama Siegel?"

Mrs. Siegel looked up. "It's Polly. They found my sweet Polly."

The other woman took a step back, put a hand over her chest, and then said, "We need Harry."

CHAPTER 11

CHARLES AARON

The constables had arrived, and he found that his worries were making him scattered. Hopefully Joseph would arrive soon and all Charles would have to worry about was Georgette and the children. Georgette was pale and shaking. He wanted to carry her up to their bed and lay her down, but he knew she would never let him. Nor would she rest when she knew there was the skeleton of a little girl in their house. The body had to go before Georgette would ever sleep.

Then, somehow, the orphans had wormed their way into his heart and worries in a few short days. What would it be like after years of caring about them? Let alone when it came to his own child. The children he had to concern himself with at the moment were still struggling over the death of their own parents.

He sighed. The workmen, Eunice, and the children had all come out to the front of the house and were watching as the constables approached where Charles and Georgette stood apart. The first introduced himself, and Charles quite missed the man's name.

"You're sure it was a body, Mr. Aaron?"

Charles almost rolled his eyes. As though he could misidentify a human skeleton, still wearing the dress she'd been murdered in. "Yes," was all he said.

"There was no question," Georgette said with a voice that was too soft and thready for Charles's liking. He knew she'd been thinking about crafting their own happily ever after. Was she letting that dream be ruined by what they'd discovered in their house? If they decided to sell, they'd never be able to get rid of it after a murdered child had been found there. "You could see a dress, and hair. The skeleton was quite obviously human."

"Did you move it or touch it?"

She shook her head and Charles took the man inside to see for himself. When they returned, Georgette described how the bed had been placed on its side over it. A sort of lean-to hiding the body. The constable cursed, apologized, and muttered darkly under his breath.

"Sweet little thing, Polly was. It must be her. We'll

have to confirm, of course, but it must be her. We've already called Scotland Yard and requested the other Mr. Aaron. It'll be best to be precise and careful when it's Polly. We all loved her, you know. We all did. We need to dot every i and cross every t."

The constable behind the first muttered, "Someone didn't love her."

Georgette stumbled a little and Charles caught her. She spoke up even though he was steadying her. "I was thinking that."

Charles closed his eyes, entirely unsurprised his love had been picking at what had happened.

"We moved boxes from in front of the beds," Georgette told the constables. "Really, when you consider the geography of the attics, it's apparent. There was the wall, then the body, then the bed that was placed at an angle over Polly, so there was no seeing her."

"That does sound deliberate," said one of the men.

"Oh," Georgette added, "you don't quite understand, I think. *Then,* there was *another* bed in front of the one at the angle. It was quite a beastly bed and covered in things. There were empty bedrooms and the bed we moved wasn't damaged. Why would you move a perfectly functional bed to the attic and leave another room empty?"

"Ah?" The constable frowned. "To hide a body?"

"We moved it all having no idea that the poor girl was a few feet away." Georgette paused. "In front of that second, very heavy bed, there was a broken dresser, a wardrobe, a good dozen boxes. It took us at least an hour just to get to the first bed, and we were working only to get there, removing boxes instead of looking through them. If we weren't heading specifically for a bed? It might have taken me weeks and weeks to get through all of that stuff to even realize the bed wasn't damaged."

"If Mr. Essent hadn't sold the house..." The constable had finally caught onto Georgette's thoughts.

"No one would have found her for quite some time." Georgette shivered and Charles wrapped his arm around her.

"This has been quite a shock for my wife," Charles said. "I don't want to be cold, but perhaps we can move the child and allow my wife to sit and have some tea before we return to the rather grim tidings?"

The constables nodded. "The other Mr. Aaron is informing Mrs. Siegel today. It needs to be done before the rumors get too far. Poor woman deserves to catch her breath and have a good cry before folks start dropping by on her."

The constables conferred quietly and the one went inside while the other crossed to the man with an ambulance.

Charles watched his Georgette shiver again with her hand slipping from the opposite elbow down to her stomach. He tugged her closer to him, hugging her tight. Their baby was fine. This poor mother would be —at the least—given the chance to bury and officially say goodbye to her daughter. Charles sighed into

Georgette's hair. It didn't seem to help all that much, and he hoped to never know for himself.

Eunice crossed to them. "I'm taking the children to the library and for a long walk."

"Take them to the pub for lunch," Georgette said, shivering.

"Is it really Polly?" Lucy asked, her hand wrapped tightly around Janey's. Poor Eddie was pale and sick-looking.

"Yes," Charles told them. "The constables will be returning her to her to family, and we'll be doing what we can to help them with their work."

"Was she murdered?" Eddie asked. "Did someone do that to her?"

"We don't know yet," Charles said. "I won't tell you it'll be all right. Not for the people who loved her. All we can do is help and be a little kinder, a little more helpful, a little better to make up for the loss that occurred here."

Lucy nodded and Janey pressed her face into Lucy's chest, but then she looked up. "Will you make us go now because of this? Will we all be too much trouble?"

"You're staying with us, Janey," Charles said. "This is your home now."

The saying of it cemented that last niggling doubt in his mind. He'd never expected to take on three nearly-grown orphans, but he wasn't sorry he had. He'd done this once before with Joseph and Robert. Charles knew already that the good outweighed the hard things.

Janey's lip was trembling again, but she nodded as she wrapped her arms around Lucy.

"They won't be sleeping in the attic now, Charles." Georgette considered for a moment and then said, "You'll take the rooms above the kitchens so Eunice can hear if you need anything."

"Those are too fine," Eddie objected, but Georgette waved him off.

Eunice looked at the children. "You'll be coming up with ideas of what we can do for the family."

"I know," Lucy said. "The vicar said the graves were overgrown because the handyman has been ill. We could make sure the Siegel graves are all cleaned up."

Eunice nodded and clucked the children after her as though they were ducklings. They went along even though they were nearly grown. It was a good plan, Charles thought, to do good for the Siegel family.

The moment the children were gone, Georgette looked up at him. "How can it be? Why would anyone hurt a girl?"

"I believe most motives tend to be the same nonsense. Greed, to hide something, love, and fury," Charles told her. "And none of them are good enough reason for what happened. Are you going to be all right staying here, Georgette?"

She nodded. "I feel certain that if there is a lingering spirit, it is a sweet thing. Perhaps Polly is still here and perhaps she wanted us to find her body. But, Charles, the evil—whatever led to her death is gone. If she stays after she is buried, and I'm not sure that she would, we'd have a guardian angel."

They went inside, finding their way to the kitchens where Georgette scrubbed her hands for far too long. While she did, Charles made the tea, having to dig through the cupboards until he found the extensive stash.

Without asking, he made her a mix of chamomile and mint tea. It had been what his mother made him when things were wrong. He added to the tea too much milk and sugar for Georgette and left his with a bit of lemon and solitary sugar cube.

She was sitting at the table, staring out the window. The garden was bright with sun shining down on the lawn, the flowers. The willow tree laid out interesting patterns on the ground. There was the sound of workmen and constables working together as they carried out furniture and boxes, loading them into the two empty bedrooms. Georgette and Charles could hear the steps overhead as they moved up and down the stairs.

"What do we do?" Georgette asked Charles. "The children are cleaning up the Siegel graves. No doubt Eunice will keep them working beyond those graves until they are hungry, tired, and ready for a bath and a bed, but what do *we* do?"

Charles wanted, he thought, to say that they'd taken in Eddie, Lucy, and Janey. Even though it was new, however, it didn't feel noteworthy. It wasn't a place to feel as though they'd done something extraordinary. It was just what they had done and would do again. Charles had little doubt that they'd never regret it.

He tangled his fingers with Georgette's. "I don't know what to do, Georgette. What can be done? There's nothing that makes up for what happened here."

Georgette sighed and sipped her tea. She didn't even seem to notice it wasn't one of her odd teas, so he found his concern growing. Could the shock affect the baby? Would they lose their little one in all of this? If they did, he had to admit he'd be more grateful they'd barely believed the baby was there before it was gone.

She rose a few minutes later, and Charles followed as Georgette walked outside, silently. Her hands trailed the flowers that grew next to the house. Her gaze moved from the house to the back gate and the wood, to the edge of their garden that bordered the Mustly garden. He didn't need her to tell him she was imagining what Polly might have seen and done.

Georgette's gaze stopped on a treehouse in the garden next door. It was on the border of the property and the vantage point from the treehouse allowed a view of both gardens. Her gaze narrowed and she moved on.

Polly could have been playing in that treehouse. She could have been swinging on the old swing they'd removed from the willow tree. She could have been walking along the path of the wood that went behind both the Mustly house and the Essent house.

She could have been doing anything. There were no answers. Nothing that would make things obvious. Nothing that would tell them what had happened to a girl, five years before, and why she had been killed and hidden.

The mystery of it was going to bother Georgette until they knew. Charles sighed. Joseph needed to find the killer before it drove Georgie batty. She tucked her arm through his and laid her head on his shoulder as they rounded the house. A rather unexpectedly handsome man with a medical bag in hand was looking down at the form on the stretcher.

"Must be Polly, of course." He looked sick at the sight of what was in front of him. "Terrible accident. Terrible thing."

The constable whose name had not filtered into Charles's subconscious stared at the doctor, jaw dropped. "This is clearly murder."

"Course it isn't. Terrible accident. Probably crawled in the attic to play and got stuck. We were busy looking for her while she was hidden in the attic."

"Look at her skull," the constable told the doctor flatly. "It has been struck by a blunt instrument. Even I can see that, and I'm no doctor."

"Probably happened after the girl died. It's been years, Higgins."

Constable Higgins snapped his jaw closed, but the disgusted look he gave the doctor had Charles wrapping his arm around Georgette.

"That man really is an idiot," Georgette told him. "How could her head have been crushed in that protected area that she was in? How did she get to the attic? Why didn't anyone hear her cry for help? Only someone who *knew* there was a body wouldn't investigate whatever scent followed."

Charles didn't try to answer any of the questions, but he thought they were all accurate. Instead he said, "We really do need to find a different doctor. This one seems to have bribed his way out of medical school."

CHAPTER 12

MARIAN PARKER

*S*omething had happened, of course it had. Joseph had told her to go to Harper's Hollow by herself. It wasn't that she objected, although her mother had. Marian didn't mind taking the train to Harper's Hollow alone. She suspected she'd be doing it time and again in the coming years. She was hardly afraid to travel alone.

It was that he hadn't told her *what* had happened. She was sitting on this train, her dog lying at her feet, and she was thinking: Was Georgette all right? Had something happened with those orphans they'd taken in? Was Charles hurt? She didn't think it would be any of those things, not if Joseph was sending her on ahead without an explanation. It had to be something else.

She pulled out her copy of *The Chronicles of Harper's Bend* and took a deep breath in. Sliding into the tale that had cemented Georgette and Marian as friends (as it gave Marian a far better idea of Georgette's nature) was just what Marian needed to occupy her mind. When she arrived in her new hometown, she would confirm that Georgette was well, that Charles was well, and that whatever had happened, they'd get through it together.

The train was rather full and Marian was pulled from her book time after time by the whispering of a large family. Four grown men, their mother, and what looked to be two wives. The men were quite obviously brothers. If you took two, side by side, they could just be friends. . The group of them together, however, proclaimed them for what they were. Two who had matching eyes. Three with the same jawline. The same thick hair in varying shades of brown. The same slight peak at their hairline. Two with quite large frames and two with somewhat more standard shapes.

"Are they *sure* it is Polly?" one of them men asked again. There was a bit of an agonized tone in his plea that had been what caught Marian's attention.

"Yes, Harry. For the love of all that is holy, stop asking Mama. She told you all she knows."

Harry shot a devil's gaze at his brother and then glanced to the other two brothers. One shook his head, not meeting anyone's gaze. He was leaning over, elbows on his knees, face in his hands. The other was staring out the window lost in thought. If Marian were to guess, she'd assume he hadn't even heard the first brother.

"Why did it have to be Polly?" Harry muttered. "Why her?"

No one answered, but the mother wiped away a tear. Her handkerchief was so sopping one of her daughters-in-law reached out and pressed a fresh one into her hand. It didn't seem to be the first time it had been done for her, and she didn't seem to notice.

"Do you remember the way she sang every morning?" This was from the one who was still staring out the window. "She was always too good for us. We should have guessed God would take her back."

The mother bit down on her bottom lip.

"Mama, do you really think it was that Yelena woman?"

She didn't answer. She laid her head against the bulky son next to her and closed her eyes. The tears continued letting them all know she was awake. Marian hated herself for staring, but she couldn't quite look away. They didn't seem to notice.

"Do you remember how good she was at making flower crowns?" It was the one by the window again. "Every time I see one, I think of her. Little Polly braiding flowers like a master of the art, singing while she did."

"*Who* would do this?" It was the angry Harry again. "Why?"

Yet again no one answered. "You sold the house, Mama?"

"You know she did, Harry. I called ahead. They have rooms for us at the Bear and Dog."

It was the house reference that clarified the picture for Marian. Somehow, this family's relative . . . sister? . . . Regardless, she had died and they were all going. Given that Joseph had been called to work in Harper's Hollow, Marian now knew why.

It made sense. Joseph had become quite chummy with the local constables. If they had a case, they'd ask for him. The kind of thing that needed more than the locals could provide.

In Harper's Hollow, Marian had heard the rumors of the missing child. It had been years since the child had gone. What had the man-of-business said? Mrs. Siegel had left because of something associated with her child. If she'd disappeared and was only now found dead, Marian could just imagine wanting to escape the bad memories. Of thinking every time someone knocked at your door, you'd learn that your child had been found down a well or under a hedge.

Mrs. Siegel must have moved away from the memories, putting her house up for sale. Marian looked down at her hands. She and Joseph had bought that house. They couldn't go home to bury their child because she and Joseph were the owners now. Only—only, they hadn't moved in yet, had they? Marian had a rather stuffed case to bring some of her things down, but those could remain at Georgette's

Taking in a deep breath, Marian let it out slowly. To think! To lose a child, sell your house, and then have the child found. Marian bit down on her bottom lip and tried, "Mrs. Siegel?"

All the women in the party looked up. Even the eldest, who met Marian's gaze with surprise and shock.

"Yes," Marian said, "I thought it might be you. I'm Marian Parker. I'm sorry. I overheard you. It was my fiancé who bought your house."

Mrs. Siegel stared blankly at Marian.

"If it would be easier for you to stay in your old house, you can. Joseph won't mind. We haven't moved a thing yet."

Mrs. Siegel blinked, wiping a stray tear off of her cheekbone. Her voice was hoarse as she said, "It would be nice. It would be nice to be home when we bury Polly."

Marian nodded. "Then you shall be." Marian slowly pulled the key out of her handbag. She hadn't let anyone take it from her since it had been left in her care, and she had not intended to let it go again. It was, however, the right thing to do, and it felt right in her head.

Mrs. Siegel didn't thank Marian, and Marian didn't expect it. Officially, the house was owned by Joseph now, but Marian knew he'd have offered to do the same.

She turned back to her book. Otherwise, their manners would nag at them to speak to her, comment on the weather, and the general state of things. She wasn't going to do that to a mourning family, so she pretended to read her book instead, and they pretended they didn't know it was a pretense. In a few minutes, the family spoke to each other again, but they whispered now and Marian wasn't able to hear their grief anymore.

~

THE WALK to Georgette's house was fraught with traffic and when Marian arrived, suitcase in hand, dog on a leash, she paused in horrified shock. Two police autos were parked behind Charles's. Seated at a small iron table that someone had moved to the side of the yard was Georgette, Charles, and another couple. Georgette was watching the police come and go.

A truck was also parked near the autos and old furniture was being piled in the garden. Marian crossed to Georgette.

"Was it you?"

"Who found her?" Georgette asked, understanding immediately. "Yes, the children and I were looking for beds. She was under one."

Marian must have paled because Charles pressed her into his chair. "Deep breath, Marian."

"Are you all right?" she demanded, ignoring Charles's suggestion.

"No," Georgette said with blithe honesty. "But I will be. Meet Mr. and Mrs. Mustly. They are our neighbors."

Marian nodded and then they fell silent. Charles returned with another chair and another cup, and Marian realized they were all sipping one of Georgette's odd teas. The usualness of Georgette with her odd teas, milky and sweet, the sight of Charles with his careful gaze on his wife, the pressure of another dead person. It was a fraught and odd world. Marian accepted her cup and drank deeply. Somehow, tea with Georgette did seem to set the world aright again.

"Should we be here?" Marian asked carefully. A large bed made of fine wood and looking as if it had been attacked with an axe was being placed on the ground by the workmen under the direction of a uniformed constable.

"There's no point in making us leave," Charles said.

"What about...evidence...maybe they can find some scrap of something to say what happened to Polly."

"We've already destroyed whatever evidence might have been obtainable before we redid the flooring and painted. If there was blood on the bottom of a carpet or remnants on a wall, it's gone now."

"People said your house was haunted, Georgette. Do you think they knew?"

Georgette shook her head. "Only a fiend would leave a mother wondering and a child unburied. Maybe they guessed? Maybe they just instinctively put together a string of little things, so they wondered, but no one took their theory seriously or she'd have been found long since. Perhaps, however, there is a spirit here."

"Georgette says if there's a spirit, it's Polly watching over us," Charles added.

"She would've," Mr. Mustly said gruffly. "Kindest,

sweetest little thing you ever saw. No need to fear her. No need for anyone to fear her. No need to hurt her either." The last was said with such utter fury that Marian flinched. Mr. Mustly didn't notice. He rose and walked away, towards and out the back gate.

"He loved her," Mrs. Mustly said. "She was the light of our lives. Our children grown and gone and little Polly coming by to putter in the garden with Barnaby or take tea and biscuits. She'd listen to our stories and ask for them over and over again, as though each time was the first time. My husband loved her with every-thing inside of him, and he's never been the same since she left us. She was a joy. She was our joy even if she wasn't ours."

Mrs. Mustly cried as silently as Mrs. Siegel. Geor-gette reached out a hand and squeezed Mrs. Mustly's even as Georgette topped off the woman's tea and pushed the tin of biscuits closer.

"What I want to know," Georgette said quietly, "is what could have caused her death. She is reported time and again as a sweet thing. How old was she?"

"Oh," Mrs. Mustly considered. "She must have been about seventeen. But you have to understand, she was quite small for her age. More like ten or eleven. But with the awareness and understanding of a small child. She didn't understand when people were angry. She didn't understand the complexities of relation-ships. To her, everyone was her friend unless she didn't like them. She was forever a child."

"She looked like a little girl?"

Mrs. Mustly nodded. "Dressed as one too. Short

dress, bows in her hair. Little locket about her neck that had a picture of her and her mother and one of her dead father. She used to open it and point out how they all looked the same."

"Why are you asking, Georgette?"

"Charles, whoever killed that child lives among us."

Mrs. Mustly gasped.

"So you have to wonder why someone would kill a girl who everyone loved because maybe they'll have a reason to do it again."

Mrs. Mustly gasped again.

Charles sighed. "The reasons are always the same, Georgette. In order to get something they want, in an act of fury or revenge, for money, or to prevent from being caught for something."

"Or to defend yourself, but I suppose that isn't really murder." Marian shivered and reached down to the dogs, petting her own dog and Bea at the same time. Georgette was still holding Mrs. Mustly's hand as she glanced between them.

"But no one would have killed Polly for money or revenge. She didn't have anything anyone could want."

"Exactly my point," Charles said, glancing at his wife.

Georgette finished, "Polly must have infuriated someone or seen something she shouldn't have. Given what you said of her, she might not have even understood what she had seen. But—"

Mrs. Mustly shook her head and then lifted her teacup with both hands, the cup trembling between her fingers. "That…that…whoever…however…I don't know. But they need to be found."

"We aren't looking for the murderer," Georgette said to Mrs. Mustly. "We'll never find them. Not if we're looking to somehow peek back in time, find the secret, and then trap the killer. It'll never happen."

"They need to pay," Mrs. Mustly said. "Eye for an eye. Life for a life. I want them to be burning in a fiery hell for what they did to my Polly."

"Oh, I agree," Georgette said. "We can't recreate the situation. The killer has hidden so well. I doubt any progress will ever be made to find the killer if we're looking for the killer. No," Georgette said simply, "we look instead for Yelena Essent's husband or lover."

CHAPTER 13

JOSEPH AARON

*H*is love was sitting next to Georgette and Charles. The look on Marian's face was horrified and shocked. The look of the old woman identified as Anna Mustly was horrified and shocked. The look on Charles's face was resigned. The look of Georgette's was musing.

Joseph shook his head. Georgette had been given *too* much time to consider upon the vagaries of mankind while people overlooked her. She'd learned to put pieces together too quickly, too easily, and quite frankly—she was too clever for Charles's, Joseph's, or Marian's own good.

Joseph crossed the green and put his hands on his hips. He stared down at Georgette and she smiled at him, offering a cup of tea. With a sigh, he accepted it and drank it down. This one had cinnamon and orange, and he had to admit he loved it. His fingers tangled with Marian's.

"Have you heard that Yelena Essent had a lover?"

It was Georgette. Of course it was Georgette. He was a little surprised she hadn't already handed him the killer.

Joseph muttered to himself and then said, "Just the rumors."

Georgette lifted her brows.

"You believe there was a lover and that he and Yelena killed Polly." Joseph didn't bother hiding his suspicions.

Georgette leaned back and met his gaze.

He shook his head in resignation. "I agree. The only people who could have put the body in the attic were Yelena and her lover. The husband was the one who destroyed the furniture. He was angry about something. Constable Higgins says that Yelena was *certainly* pregnant just before she died. They looked into her death, confirmed that it was likely the result of an abortion, and let it go. There was so much grief at the time about Polly. Mr. Essent was a proud and very rich man who had done much for the community. The constables didn't want to make him uncomfortable"

"How far apart were the events?"

"The constable intends to look it up to confirm, but he thinks no more than a month or two."

Mrs. Mustly frowned. "Polly Siegel disappeared on March 17th, five years ago."

Joseph stared.

"We loved her," Mrs. Mustly said. "We looked for her for months and months after she was gone. My husband still does. Or did. I had to stop. I couldn't take it anymore. Every year on that date, however, we would braid flower chains and have a picnic in our garden. I'm not ashamed to say we end it crying every time. Both of us."

Georgette wiped away a sympathy tear as did his love, Marian. She was the most beautiful thing he'd ever seen and it shone from her particularly brightly when her kindness and love was so very clear. He needed to thank God daily for giving him such a love.

"Why a picnic and flower chain?" he asked.

"That was what we did with Polly," Mrs. Mustly said. "The last day, she came by early and asked to bake with me. We started by baking biscuits, bread, and sweet rolls. While the bread and rolls were raising, we took the warm biscuits with some meat pies to the garden with Barnaby. Polly braided us flower crowns, and we wore them while we sipped our ginger beer and had our lunch. I went in, but Barnaby stayed with her. They had been watching a mother sparrow from her meeting her fellow to building the nest. They'd spend hours watching her, finding different bugs, catching frogs. They came in just before teatime, and we scrubbed Polly up and sent her home for tea. We never saw her again."

"What a lovely memory," Georgette said.

"So somewhere between your garden and her home, she saw something. Yelena Essent is the clear suspect here with whomever she was with." Joseph frowned. "Do you remember when Yelena Essent died?"

"It was May," Mrs. Mustly told them. "I can't remember which day, but I remember it was May because she died after May Day. I spoke to her on May Day about how much Polly loved that day, just in passing you know. She said that Polly was better off in heaven than being useless here." Mrs. Mustly smiled wickedly. "I slapped her. As hard as I've ever slapped anyone, and I slapped my boys a good one a time or two. I slapped her and my only regret is that I didn't do more."

"Mrs. Mustly." Georgette topped off everyone's tea and then frowned when the teapot emptied, but then gave Mrs. Mustly a bright smile. "I knew I liked you."

"She's my new favorite human," Marian said.

"All right," Joseph said, taking the chair that Charles handed over. Charles went for another while Joseph sketched out a timeline. He frowned at the timeline and then shook his head. "You know what she might have seen?"

"Yelena and her lover together. If it were the husband," Georgette said, succinctly illustrating Joseph's thoughts, "there wouldn't have been a reason to kill the little girl. You'd just walk her home and have a talk with the mother."

"What happened to the housekeeper the Essents used?"

Mrs. Mustly paused. "Morry? I don't know. I can find out."

"See if you can. I'll put the local boys on it as well," Joseph said. "Georgette, whoever killed that child will kill again. If you kill over an assignation, you'd kill to hide a murder."

"Stay out of it," Charles told Georgette. "That's what he's saying. You and Marian both."

"We live here," Georgette told them both innocently.

"Also," Marian added, "she can't just stop using her mind. It darts ahead with or without your permission."

"Be careful then," Joseph muttered. "Stay together. Stick with Mrs. Mustly or the people we don't suspect. Just be careful."

～

CHARLES AARON

The thing about Georgette was that she could not, in fact, stop thinking. She had picked at the problem of the murder and thought out that it must be Yelena Essent and whoever had helped her before Charles had even considered upon the matter. He'd fallen in love with her because of her mind. He thought she was beautiful, but he'd become consumed by the way her mind worked, the way there were worlds behind her honey-brown eyes.

It wasn't possible for her to only be clever when it was convenient and safe.

"We need a telephone."

Georgette glanced up, surprised. "It's on our list, isn't it?"

"Now. I think we need one now." He pressed a kiss on her forehead and said his goodbyes. He needed to get the telephone installed in the house, he needed to call his partner and let Luther know that he would be working from the house for the next while, and he needed Robert to bring rather a lot of work down, so Charles's partner didn't revolt.

Charles caught a ride to the main part of town with one of the constables and then arranged for the telephone, having the constable come in and put pressure on the fellow to move quickly 'for Polly.'

Charles was fine with the telephone being used to help Polly. However, he wanted his Georgette to be able to call for help. While he was there, he used their telephone to call his partner who muttered about Death and his tendency of striking while Georgette was near.

"I'll be sending you all the work I don't want to do."

"Understandable," Charles said without objection. "Luther, my friend, if we were to publish this in a book, no one would believe it. How many deaths are going to occur around us before they stop?"

"I believe you just jinxed your life, my friend."

"Don't say such things."

"It wasn't me, it was you. Throw salt over your shoulder immediately. I'm not really sure how that works. Have the vicar bless your house? You need to do something immediately, my friend. I don't mind you working from home, however, as long as you meet with the authors and do all the worst work."

"You're all generosity," Charles said. "Send Robert down, please."

"Certainly." So Charles would hear, Luther said loudly, "Robert, make sure you get the letter from Hannah Cate about her royalties and bring the ledgers, so he can explain—again—why her payment is what it is."

Charles heard Robert's assent.

"Good day, Charles," Luther finished. The last thing Charles heard was Luther's wicked laugh.

CHAPTER 14

GEORGETTE DOROTHY AARON

Georgette was sure she was seeing Polly's mother, Mrs. Siegel, even before Mrs. Mustly rose and rushed across the garden. The woman had come in the back gate with two men following. One had ruffled hair as if he'd run his hands through it so much that it could only stand on end. The other moved so brittlely, Georgette thought he must be holding in a breakdown by a sheer force of will.

The larger of the two sons picked up Mrs. Mustly and squeezed her tightly. She oomphed and demanded, "Put me down, Harry."

To the second son, she said, "Hello, Liam dear."

He nodded and his jaw tightened. It took him a

moment to unbend enough to hug Mrs. Mustly and when he did, she whispered into his ear. He nodded, eyes closed, and when he let her go and stood again, he'd kept his eyes closed. Finally, he turned away, curled into his hands for a moment, and gathered himself.

"He needs to just cry," Marian said. "I wish he would just cry."

"He might," Georgette said. "Later. Or perhaps he'll go find a punching bag and beat his hands bloody. Men are so busy being manly they forget they love too."

The two men and two women talked for a few minutes and then they crossed to where Georgette and Marian had waited. The dogs' tails thumped against the ground and Mrs. Siegel started.

"Miss Parker?"

Marian nodded and introduced everyone, telling Georgette what she had done.

"We were hoping to see…"

Georgette bit down on her bottom lip. The workmen had left with the last of the constables. Joseph had gone with them to the station. There was only Georgette and Marian at the house with Mrs. Mustly. Slowly, Georgette rose.

"I'll need to get the other key. Joseph took the one to the attic, I'm sure." She glanced among the family. "We can't disturb whatever they were doing."

They all nodded. Georgette led them inside the house, took the key from Eunice's ring in the kitchens and then led them up the staircases. Georgette desperately wanted to ask if they had known who Yelena's lover had been, but instead she only unlocked the attic door.

"Will you tell us how you found her?" Mrs. Siegel's voice was hoarse.

Georgette described the boxes, the beds, the dressers, the multitude of furniture blocking Polly in. The nursery was nearly empty now. Boxes and trunks had been stacked tightly in one of the other bedrooms. Anything broken had been taken to the garden to be disposed of in the coming days either by fire or by removal.

The entire side of the nursery, which had been loaded with so many things it had been impassable, was empty. Half the windows had been washed by Eunice and Janey, so light filtered in showing the dust. There were so many trails through the dust made by the constables, the doctor, and the workmen that it highlighted exactly how long it had been since anyone had disturbed the attic.

"Morry wouldn't have brought Polly up here," Harry said. "Right, Liam?"

"Morry was a good old broad," Liam ground out. "They hid her. They did her, didn't they?"

Harry's answer was a curse.

"The constable said she was dead when they put her in here," Mrs. Siegel said. "She wasn't afraid. She'd have been afraid otherwise." Mrs. Siegel spoke as if she were exhausted and Georgette felt certain that she was worn through. She must feel like a dishrag. Used for too long and wrung out over and over again. "He said she must have died very quickly with it over in a moment."

Harry cursed again. He cursed a streak so blue and vicious, unlike anything that Georgette had ever heard before. His brother, however, crossed to the wall and slammed his fist into it. Once, twice. Then over and over again. Both fists as fast as he could go until Mrs. Mustly stepped between him and the wall, wrapping her arms around him.

He cried for long minutes and no one said a word. It was heart-breaking. Worse perhaps than when Mrs. Siegel cried. He seemed to be weeping as though he hadn't cried since he was a child. For Polly, for his mother, for himself. For what had happened.

After a while, with Mrs. Mustly running her fingers through his hair, she said, "It's not your fault, Liam."

"You don't understand," Liam said, his words muffled by her shoulder. "You don't understand."

"It's not your fault, Liam. It's not your fault." Mrs. Mustly's voice had gone from gentle to firm.

Liam pulled back, red-faced and hollow-eyed. "You don't understand." Before Mrs. Musty could scold him again, he added, "I was her lover. I—I—was Yelena Essent's lover."

Georgette did not react while everyone else stared with dropped mouths. Mrs. Siegel was frowning, Harry was stupefied. Marian's face was carefully smooth. Mrs. Mustly was utterly and completely silent.

It was Georgette who sliced through the tension. "When?"

Liam answered as if he didn't understand why she was asking. "Ah, from when I finished school to when I took my first position in London. Ten months or so? Ten months sleeping with the woman who contributed to sweet Polly's death."

"Which was when?" They all needed precision.

"About seven years ago."

Georgette nodded. So Yelena had a long history of being unfaithful. Given her husband's reaction in the master bedroom and to the bed, had he known?

"Did her husband know about you?"

Liam shook his head, self-loathing on his face.

"Liam," Georgette said carefully, "I know you regret the Essent woman, but let me be clear—your information may just help us find your sister's killer."

He blinked at her, stunned.

"Did she have other lovers when you were with her?"

Liam nodded, jaw clenching. The self-loathing hadn't faded, but there was a dawning light of hope in his eyes.

"Do you know who they were?"

He shook his head.

"Do you know how many there were?"

He shook his head again and then said, "She had a regular lover. Every Tuesday and Thursday."

Georgette had so many more questions, but Liam was glancing with shame at his mother, and quite frankly,

Charles might strangle her if he realized she'd questioned a man about his lover. Instead she said, "Detective Inspector Aaron will want to talk to you about every detail of her that you can think of. Dredge it all up."

He swallowed thickly.

"Then let it go. What were you? Twenty or so?"

He nodded.

"Yelena Essent was a conniving woman who was clearly a skilled manipulator."

"She was," Mrs. Mustly said. "You didn't have a chance against her. Not with her wiles and your youth. You were just another of her victims. Now you know what kind of woman to avoid when you're ready to settle down."

Liam shook his head and rushed out of the attic. He was followed by his brother who, for the first time, seemed almost kind. Mrs. Mustly glanced at Mrs. Siegel and then followed the boys with Marian trailing.

Georgette didn't feel right leaving the mother in the attic alone, even if she deserved the time to say goodbye. She stood in the doorway and watched as Mrs. Siegel knelt where her daughter's body had been found. She pressed her hand onto the ground and Georgette said nothing as Mrs. Siegel curled over her knees and wept.

Long, long, long minutes passed while Mrs. Siegel succumbed to her grief and Georgette wept along with her. Finally, the woman pushed up onto her knees, wiping her face with her handkerchief. She glanced at

Georgette and then back at the spot where her daughter had lain.

Mrs. Siegel's head tilted slowly. She leaned just a little forward and then she crawled, reaching out.

"Wait!" Georgette called.

"I think...I think it's my Polly's locket."

Georgette hurried across the floor and said, "No. Don't."

"But—"

"Mrs. Siegel, that locket is so far from where the body was that someone might have touched it."

"But—it's in the crack between the wall and the floor."

"Exactly," Georgette said. "She was already dead when she was carried up here. Someone must have thrown it after her."

"I would like to have it."

"Fingerprints, Mrs. Siegel. Fingerprints. If it was thrown by the lover instead of Polly or Yelena, we might have proof of who killed your daughter."

Mrs. Siegel snatched her hand back. Her gaze was wide.

"If we can figure out who we *think* it is, that locket might be the proof we need to cement the case."

"Do you think so?"

"I think it's possible. Come, let's go out of here. Say *nothing*. This village is infected with rumors. To no one. Please."

Mrs. Siegel nodded. "I can keep a secret if it helps find the animal who hurt my girl. He needs to be burning with Yelena. That whore. Did you see what she did to my Liam? He'll carry that forever. If I could curse her to hell, I would, but I have little doubt she's suffering."

Mrs. Siegel's gaze was narrow and cold. Her hands were fisted, and her jaw was clenched. At Georgette's look, she said, "You never stop being a mother, Mrs. Aaron. They don't stop being your babies because they're adults with jobs and lives that don't include you. You worry and pray and hope and counsel and do what you can. You can't battle for them, but you can hate for them and love with them. If you can go to hell for hating, I'll be joining Yelena Essent there someday, and I won't even regret it. I'd burn myself just to see her suffer."

"Ahhh," Georgette said stupidly and then ushered the woman out of the attic. Locking it carefully behind them, they made their way down the stairs.

"Thank you," Mrs. Siegel said. She glanced around and found only Marian.

"Your sons left and Mrs. Mustly said she was going to find her husband. May I walk you home?"

Mrs. Siegel shook her head. "I thought being there would be better than anywhere else, and it is, but I keep seeing her there."

"What is she doing?"

Mrs. Siegel blinked slowly and then said, "Braiding flowers. Spinning under the trees. Singing in the window seat."

"Those seem like lovely memories." Marian's voice was gentle and careful, probably hoping to avoid offense for someone who was suffering.

Mrs. Siegel nodded, eyes tearing. "They are. They are. You're right. I'll just...go."

Georgette and Marian watched her leave and then looked at each other.

"I need tea," Marian said. "I can't imagine."

Georgette nodded, placing her hand on her stomach and Marian gasped.

"You aren't?"

"I—"

"You are!"

"I...it's early days. Nothing is sure."

"You are! I know you are." Marian threw herself at Georgette and trilled, "I'm going to be an auntie!"

"Tea," Georgette ordered with the breath she had left. The rest had been squeezed out by Marian. "Tea and perhaps I can...I don't know. I'm not good in the kitchen and Eunice is distracting the children."

"I am," Marian said. "Let's go."

They found prepared chickens in the icebox, so it was easy to peel potatoes and carrots and line a roasting pan. Marian did all the work, ordering Georgette around. They discussed baby names and the future as though a body hadn't been found earlier that day in the attic. It was what Georgette needed and when Eunice and the children returned, Marian was just pulling the food from the oven.

Eunice took in the sight of Georgette wearing an apron and laughed. "There wasn't enough chicken for all of us."

"We just made a whole bunch of potatoes," Georgette said. "Joseph and Charles will be coming along with us, but we can fill in the holes with bread and veg, right?"

"Right," Eddie said. His eyes were hollow. "Was it really Polly?"

Georgette nodded.

"She went to primary school with me before it was clear she couldn't keep up. I used to bring her little treats. I've missed her."

Georgette squeezed his arm. "Eddie darling, she knew you loved her. That's all we can look for when we lose someone we care about. That they knew we loved them and that we can be assured of their love. Take solace in that and know that Joseph will find the killer."

After the children went to wash up, Eunice said, "Joseph will find the killer?"

Marian's grin was wide as she added, "With a little help from us."

CHAPTER 15

There were times when the goddess Atë wanted to turn Georgette's head. Think, Atë wanted to say, look. Look! Look and see! You aren't thinking about what you should be thinking about and because of it someone else will die.

But, of course, that would ruin the fun. Instead Atë moved her wily eye from the grieving family. Too wholesome to watch for long, though Atë did enjoy a good vicious mother.

From the mother with the fire in her breast to the Joseph Aaron who had also been consumed by the minutia of the investigation. He was tracking down Mr. Essent. He was having a Yard doctor look at Polly Siegel after half a conversation with Dr. Fowler. He was having a constable read the old case notes to have them list out everyone who said they'd seen Polly that day, and he was fighting with himself about bringing home the case notes. Georgette's gaze, he knew, would be highly invaluable and highly irregular. A conundrum.

Charles Aaron was less interesting. He had adjusted to the father role. It slipped onto him easily because of the nephews he'd already half-raised. The orphans plus the possibility of a child? He was all lists and organizing. A tutor for Eddie, a mentor for Lucy, someone to walk with Janey until she stopped flinching quite so often. The things his own child might need. There was, in fact, a baby. If Atë focused hard enough, she'd see glimpses of the future, but really—Atë wasn't one to flip to the end of a book to discover the killer before the journey had been wrought, but she could see some things without trying: the color of the child's eyes, the nature of its personality, all the lines of mischief. But seeing mischief was, of course, as natural to her as seeing the sun in the sky.

From Charles, Atë turned her eyes to the killer. Oh, he was fun to watch. Pacing, hands in his hair. All for naught. And Yelena dead. They couldn't find him. They couldn't. No one knew he'd been dipping in the Essent pot. Except—except...oh. Loose ends needed to be wrapped up, mouths needed to be closed. He wouldn't lose everything. Bloody hell, he wouldn't lose anything.

JOSEPH AARON

Joseph would have liked to be surprised that Georgette found something that his men hadn't. He would
have liked to have been surprised by her handing him
a source of information in the Siegel son and former
lover that would be invaluable. He would like to have
been surprised that she seemed to be two steps ahead
of him, but the only thing that surprised him was that
Marian was such an excellent chef.

He was, he had to admit, guilty of assuming she
couldn't cook. He had resigned himself to a few years
of terrible dinners until she learned. Even if Eunice
had done half the prep of this bird, however, it was
moist on the inside, crisp on the outside, and the veg
that they'd served to go along with it were better
roasted potatoes than he'd have expected.

Eunice and the children had already eaten in the
kitchens when Joseph ate, but Georgette suggested he
discuss Polly with Eddie, and Joseph had little doubt
that he'd discover something about Polly that would
help. If at the same time, Georgette's aim of aiding the
boy by getting him to help also worked, Joseph would
not be surprised.

Joseph ate, then joined Eddie in the library where
the boy was staring out the window instead of pouring
over his books. Joseph sat down with two cups of
coffee, handing one to Eddie. He might have added a
little whiskey to his and a Georgette level of milk and
sugar to Eddie's, but the boy noted they both had a
cup and sat up a little straighter.

"Georgette tells me you knew Polly well."

"I did." Eddie clenched his jaw and then sipped the coffee. He frowned a little and Joseph snorted.

"Georgette tells me you visited her. Did you see her on the day she died?"

Eddie shook his head. "I'd go by when I didn't have school work and my parents didn't need me for anything. You could bring her anything. Anything at all. A pretty rock and she'd be thrilled. If I found something she'd like, I'd bring it to her. She had a little chest hidden in that treehouse Mr. Mustly fixed up for her. I'd bring her something for it, and she'd show me her treasures."

Joseph paused for a moment and then asked, "Where was it?"

"The treasure chest?"

Jospeh nodded.

"Oh, in her tree house. There's a little box to sit on, but Mr. Mustly made it a bit like a puzzle box. It pulls apart if you know how to do it."

Joseph stretched his neck and took a deep drink of the coffee. "Did Polly fear anyone?"

"She didn't really get scared. She couldn't hold onto it. She just liked people or didn't like them. If she didn't like them, she avoided them. If she liked them, she'd light up when they approached."

"Who didn't she like?"

The boy scratched the back of his neck and ran his hand through his hair. Joseph liked him. He'd heard his story, winced for all three of the kids. But there was something in Eddie's gaze and the way he talked, the way he thought carefully before he answered that reflected in him as a solid and kind young man.

"She didn't like Yelena Essent. Not at all. Polly always used to stop and scowl towards the house. Yelena had found Polly using the back gate from her house to shortcut to the Mustly's and had chased her out of the garden like she was a thief."

"Did she shortcut often?"

"Whenever she had a new dress she liked or she had special instructions not to get dirty. The Mustlys have a stone wall between them and the wood. There isn't a gate, so she had to climb it. It wasn't like Polly hurt anything cutting through the garden. She just opened the gate and hurried through. Why the fuss?"

Joseph didn't answer, but he could guess given what he was hearing about Yelena Essent's pastimes. Joseph changed the subject, asking Eddie about his dream, his parents. The boy teared up and then he asked, "Do you think that Charles and Georgette will really let us stay here? They won't get...over...helping us?"

"I can't see them letting you leave at all, Eddie. Maybe it's because Georgette has been talking about spirits lately that they're on my mind. If you believe in them, you should believe your parents guided the Aarons to you and your sisters. Charles raised me after my parents died. I was about your age. You can trust them. Both of them. They both know what it's like to be without parents, and they're kind. I'm sure many others would have helped you but couldn't afford to do so. Georgette and Charles won't be burdened by feeding you too."

Eddie nodded and then glanced down at his books with a sigh.

"It's all right to take the evening off."

"I don't want to let them down."

"You won't."

Eddie nodded and left the room with a novel under his arm rather than his school books. Before he left, however, he carefully stacked up his notes and school books, putting them away. It looked as though he'd never been there when he disappeared to the kitchens and up the back steps.

∾

GEORGETTE DOROTHY AARON

Georgette couldn't sleep, and she couldn't write. She'd have woken Charles, but he was awake too, sitting up in bed, making notes in his book. He was muttering about things like tutors and cradles.

Georgette kissed his cheek and told him she was going for tea, but he just nodded, frowning at his book. In the kitchen, she put a pot of tea on the burner and turned to see Marian and Joseph sitting in the dark.

Georgette gasped, clutching her chest, and then muttered about imagining spirits too much. "Do you want me to leave?"

The shadows of their heads shook. They had been

whispering by the light of the moon and the hall light, so Joseph reached out and flipped on the kitchen light, making all of them wince.

"We're just dreaming," Marian said, still holding Joseph's hand.

Georgette nodded. "I can't sleep. Something is niggling at my mind and I can't figure it out."

"Me too," Joseph said, frowning. "This isn't good."

Georgette shook her head and silently padded back to the sink to add more water to the teapot. "Did you learn anything?"

"Just that Polly used the Essent garden for a shortcut as often as not."

It wasn't surprising, so she just nodded and then opened the cabinet where her tea hoard was housed. She opened canisters, sniffed, and then returned them, finally settling on one with a slightly toffee scent.

Georgette brought down the large mugs, bypassing the pretty tea cups they usually used, and set the tea to steeping.

"It was heart-wrenching watching Mrs. Siegel weep over where her daughter had been left today. I keep thinking about it. Let alone when Liam—well, I suppose the less discussed the better." Georgette took in deep breaths of the steeping tea. "Whoever killed Polly Siegel is a monster."

"Unfortunately you can't distinguish monsters from everyone else most of the time." Joseph was playing with Marian's fingers as Georgette made the tea. She handed them both mugs and then Joseph said almost hesitantly, "My case notes and the file are in Charles's office."

He didn't expand upon it and Georgette filled her large mug with her favorite tea and disappeared down the hall. Did she find her way to the office? Of course she did.

It was 3:00 a.m. when Georgette finished reading the police notes and Joseph's notes, and she'd discovered nothing. Little details but nothing. She'd even dug through the stacks of old Essent's ledgers and files that Charles had set aside and mostly found things about a factory with a few household bills. Nothing, nothing, and more nothing. She was staring out the window of Charles's office when he came into the room and put his hands on his hips.

"What is this, Mrs. Aaron? Are you stepping out on me with murder?"

She nodded.

"Did you learn anything?"

She shook her head.

"You won't be able to process it exhausted, my love." He tugged her to her feet and pulled her from the office, up the stairs, and almost shoved her into bed. She settled against his side, tangled their fingers together, and said, "It's just nicer with you around."

He pressed a kiss on her forehead. "Go to sleep."

"I love you."

Her proclamation was echoed and then she was chased into sleep by the warmth of his body calming hers.

CHAPTER 16

JOSEPH AARON

*M*r. Essent was a large man. Joseph could immediately picture him with an axe destroying the master bedroom in his house. He had dark, thick eyebrows and quite dark eyes. Not just dark in color—though they were—but dark in view. It was as if there was no light in them at all, but there was not the slightest indication in any of Joseph's senses that the man was a murderer.

"You're here about the child?" Mr. Essent said. "I assumed you would be."

He had a deluxe set of rooms in London with a solitary manservant who had opened the door. Joseph was seated on a leather buttoned chair across from

Mr. Essent, who was in a chair so large it looked to have been custom made for his bulk.

"I am here about Polly Siegel."

"I heard she was found in the house. Those poor fools who bought the house. Was it a servant who found it?"

Joseph shook his head. "It was Mrs. Aaron."

"The lady of the house?" Mr. Essent's scowl deepened. "I suppose given the low offer they gave me they can't really afford a house of that size. Are they trying to keep it up themselves?"

Joseph wasn't there to comment on his uncle's income and honestly, given Georgette's books were becoming more and more well-liked, he didn't think they were struggling. Joseph rubbed the back of his neck. "Regardless. What can you tell me about Polly Siegel?"

"She was a sweet little thing. I used to give her sweets when I was home. I don't know how she got there, but I wouldn't, would I?"

"Why wouldn't you?"

"I was in Bournemouth. My factory had a fire. We lost too many workers and quite a bit of our stock. I was there for weeks sorting things out. I remember hearing about it on the train on the way home. She was lost in March. She'd been gone for weeks when I got home, but I still walked the wood a good half-dozen times with Mustly."

"You heard about it on the train?"

"Ran into a fellow from home on the train. We rode back together. My wife didn't tell me if that's what you mean. But of course she wouldn't have. She knew where Polly was—must've."

"Do you really think so?"

"There was no way to hide a body in the attic and her not know. It must have smelled. Must've. Morry, bless her, had the senses of a dead dog. I used to tell Yelena that if there was a fire, we'd have to go get the old girl and drag her out. Morry would never have known herself."

"There was only Yelena?"

"Yelena, Morry, a daily girl who Yelena fired as often as she hired a new one. It was an endless cycle of terrified seventeen-year-olds scrubbing the floor. I used to make excuses for her, but she was a ripe, loud, spoilt, cruel…well, witch. The only servant we kept for very long was Morry, and I'll be damned if it wasn't because she was near deaf and couldn't hear the mean things Yelena would say."

Joseph leaned back. "You don't sound as if you miss her."

"Why would I? I was besotted. I adored her. I gave her anything she wanted, and I came home to her half-dead in bed with blood between her legs. When she told me what happened, well—it was an abortion all right. Some fool with a hacksaw by the look of it. I can't have children since the war, and I'd been gone with the fire anyway. There wasn't even the chance that she could have lied and said it was a miracle."

"What happened?" Joseph asked. His stomach was roiling. Mr. Essent had a way with words and Joseph could picture all too easily what happened to the man's wife.

"Called for the doctor. It was too late. Nothing to be done. Infection had set in. She had a fever. He did what he could, but she was dead in all but fact by the time I'd found her."

"Did anyone come around? Anyone at all who could give us an idea of who your wife's lover was?"

"Yelena had a weekly tea with some ladies in town, but never at our house. Mrs. Mustly might know if Yelena was close to anyone. She suffered from the megrims. The doctor came in regularly, though, I can't imagine Yelena confided in a man. Yelena had an odd fondness for the vicar's wife. If she were kind to anyone, it was that woman."

Joseph lifted his brows and made a note.

"Not that Yelena would tell a good woman about her liaisons. Not a fan of Oddington and his wife m'self, but Yelena liked the vicar's wife well enough."

Jospeh leaned back and waited to see if Mr. Essent would add to the tale. Perhaps with time and silence, he'd fill it in?

It didn't work. Finally Mr. Essent said, "Are you waiting for something more?"

"Is there anything more?"

Mr. Essent scoffed. "If I had an idea of what was happening with Yelena, I'd have thrown her out, divorced her, and left her penniless. I was so angry when she died that I destroyed much of my own house. If I had known who her lover was, I would have wrung his neck. I would have wrung his neck and hung his corpse outside of my house as a warning to those who cuckold and betray."

Joseph cleared his throat and shifted. He didn't think that Essent was involved in the death. The truth was, Joseph had confirmed much of Essent's accounts of his whereabouts before he'd come so he'd know whether Essent were a liar.

"But given that you weren't called to my home five years ago," Essent added, "you'll see that I remain a blind, cuckolded fool."

Slowly Joseph rose and started to leave after thanking Mr. Essent for his time. Joseph paused on the threshold of Mr. Essent's living room. "What about Morry? What happened to her?"

"I fired her, didn't I? Yelena wasn't a woman to have a tryst in the bushes. Morry either knew who the lover was or she was willingly oblivious and that's not what I paid the old bird for."

"Do you know where I can find her?"

Mr. Essent shook his head and then paused. "The vicar's wife might know. She gave Morry a place to stay, I think, after I threw her out."

GEORGETTE DOROTHY AARON

Mabel Oddington opened the door to the vicarage, noted the children along with Georgette and Marian and said, "Oh! I have been missing you."

She hugged each of the children so tightly they had

the breath squeezed from them. Eddie lifted a basket as did Lucy and Marian, and Mrs. Oddington glanced between them curiously.

"It's for the sick children," Janey said. "Georgette says we must do what we can for them."

Mrs. Oddington nodded and glanced behind her. "I'm afraid I can't deliver the food just yet."

Lucy glanced at Georgette. "We've had scarlet fever."

"Then you should deliver it," Georgette said. "Where shall we send it, Mrs. Oddington?"

Recommendations were made and the young people left. The vicar's wife watched them go and then asked, "Would you like to come in?"

Georgette and Marian took the offer and followed the woman to her kitchen where they were put to work peeling potatoes while they chatted with her. "The Lord's work is never done."

Neither Georgette nor Marian objected, so Mrs. Oddington relaxed into the things she was doing. "Are you really going to help Eddie become a doctor?"

"It seems like we can never have too many good doctors. He seems bright enough to be successful."

"But he's not your child," Mrs. Oddington said. "Surely you could just help him find a good position. Doctoring can go to someone else who has better connections."

"He's mine now," Georgette told Mrs. Oddington. "To be honest, I'd like to see him come back here to doctor."

"Doctor Fowler is quite a young man still. I don't

know that Harper's Hollow can support two doctors. No, no. Better he get a good job he can do now. The vicar was looking into a factory that might take him."

"Ah," Georgette said kindly, glancing at Marian. "Perhaps Eddie will work, *as a doctor,* somewhere else then. We were wondering if you know where we might find Morry? Who used to work at Essent house?"

Mrs. Oddington glanced between them. "May I ask why?"

Georgette considered and then flat-out lied. "We found some things that belonged to her when we were cleaning out a cupboard and would like to see she gets them."

"Oh, of course. She went to live with a brother in Ely."

"Ely? Wonderful," Georgette replied. "Do you happen to remember the brother's name?"

"Morry. It was their last name. Hers was Joan. His was Joe."

"Thank you," Georgette replied. "We had better get to the rest of the things we have to do today."

As they closed the gate to the vicarage, Marian said, "You lied in the house of God."

"That wasn't the house of God."

"Sure it was," Marian shot back.

"No." Georgette shook her head fiercely. "It's merely the...ah...dormitory for the house of God. Entirely separate. Completely different. Besides, Mrs. Oddington wouldn't have told us. She was being weird today, don't you think? She seemed different the last few times I spoke to her."

Marian shrugged. "I have no idea, and I'm not bothered by your white lie. Mrs. Oddington should have guessed why we wanted to talk to Morry. We'll tell Joseph, he'll track her down, and then—"

"Or—"

Marian paused hesitantly. "Or?"

Georgette grinned wickedly. "We could just...slip over to Ely. It isn't that far by train. We could be back before afternoon tea if we're quick."

"Charles is staying home to keep you safe. You know he is. He won't like it."

"I just want to talk to her. This Morry woman isn't going to be dangerous. She's a little old lady everyone describes as deaf. What is it called when you don't smell things easily?"

"We're not investigators," Marian tried.

Georgette just grinned wickedly again. She laughed at Marian's shocked response. "Morry will probably tell us more than she would Joseph. We're ladies. Women talk to women more easily. Really," Georgette said, making it up on the spot, "we're doing him a favor."

"He's going to wring our necks after he shakes us stupid."

"We're probably already stupid." Georgette adjusted her cloche, grabbed Marian's hand, and pulled her along to the train. "If there's an easy train, we'll do it. If there isn't, we'll tell Joseph where she is."

Marian didn't object, which Georgette took as a

whole-hearted endorsement. The next train was coming quickly and would, in fact, be an easy stop in Ely. Marian sighed and followed Georgette onto the train.

"Our future definitely includes tight jaws and stressed looks."

"Don't be dramatic," Georgette told Marian. "Charles will probably just hug me extra tight. Joseph is the jaw-flexer."

CHAPTER 17

*E*ly was beautiful. Georgette could have happily lived here, she thought. The cathedral pulled both women to a full stop even though they'd both seen it before. It was shockingly lovely, a masterpiece of stone and glass.

"I could have easily lived here," Georgette told Marian. "Why didn't we move here?"

Marian snorted and shook her head. "Living in Ely was for the type of woman who wasn't going to find a body in the attic. That's not you."

"Why not?" Georgette demanded. "I could be that person!"

"Your fate is certainly to end up in a village where there is the body of a child in the attic, and a vicar's wife who thinks your orphan isn't good enough to become a doctor. Normal people, with normal fates, live in Ely. I don't think either of us qualify anymore."

Georgette found the post office and asked after Joe and Joan Morry. She found the set of rooms not far from the train station and stopped in shock when the door was open. She had knocked and it swung slowly in. There was a creak as it moved and Georgette shivered, glancing behind her at Marian.

"Oh my goodness," Georgette said. "Hello? Hello? Morry?"

"This is…"

"This feels bad," Georgette finished as Marian took hold of her.

"Yes," Marian replied, her fingers digging into Georgette's wrist.

"Hello?" Georgette called again. "Morry?" She closed her eyes, took a deep breath, and then tried, "Anybody home?"

There wasn't an answer, but Georgette slowly stepped inside. "Morry? Morry, your door was open."

She paused a moment later, her gaze slowly registering what she was seeing. Georgette had imagined in her mind some sweet little old lady, possibly wearing a lace cap on her head, and a little fragile.

No. The woman was large. Her forearms were the size of Georgette's calves. She took up every inch of the large chair where she was sitting. Her head was leaned back, eyes open and bulging with bruising around her neck.

Marian's scream echoed through the little set of rooms, and they both backed up frantically. When they reached the doorway, someone had come running.

"Everything all right?"

Marian shook her head over and over again. Georgette leaned against the wall to keep from falling down.

"Call the constables," Georgette stuttered. "Call the doctor. Oh my goodness."

The man glanced between them, frowning.

"There's been a terrible accident," Marian said.

"There's been a murder," Georgette corrected and sat quickly down, putting her head between her knees. "Oh my goodness. Oh my goodness."

The fellow took a quick look and then yelled, "Oy! Jebby! Get the constables." He bypassed Georgette on the stairs and then came back looking as sick as Georgette felt. He sat down a few steps below Georgette and said, "That ain't right. That ain't right."

The constable came running just as Georgette felt she might be safe enough to stand. "What's all this?"

The first man answered while Georgette risked standing. She slowly took a deep breath in. "Her name is Joan Morry."

The constable cursed and rushed inside. There was another, deeper curse and he returned. "Well. Let's figure this thing out."

He questioned them extensively and when Georgette explained what happened in Harper's Hollow and that they were trying to ask her a few questions the constable's jaw dropped. "You aren't police women?"

"Ah," Georgette shook her head. "No."

"So, you're meddling."

"Yes," Georgette said without flinching. She should have flinched, she knew. She should have apologized, but she wasn't going to. She felt almost faint and that she might also weep. She hadn't been like this the last time she'd found a body. What was happening to her?

"Is there anyone who can corroborate your story?"

"Detective Inspector Joseph Aaron," Georgette said. "He works for Scotland Yard and is helping with the case there. If you call the police office in Harper's Hollow, they'll tell you."

"This Aaron know you're here?" the constable demanded.

"He won't be surprised," Marian told him, sounding sick.

The constable shook his head, cursed, and then spat on the ground. He sniffed and then cleared his throat. "You—" He shook his head again and muttered, "Don't go anywhere."

"I think even Charles is going to be upset," Marian told Georgette flatly. "Joseph and Charles both."

"We aren't children," Georgette told Marian. Children! She was feeling differently because of the baby. Georgette felt a rush of relief even as she added, "We don't have to ask for permission."

"You keep calling Lucy a child. I'm two years older than she is. I don't think it's a matter of being a child or not. It's being loved. We left, we didn't tell them, we went somewhere we assumed was safe, but knew they wouldn't like it. When you love someone, and they love you—you tell them when you're doing something ill-advised and stupid just as if you'd tell them you were going to be late or if you're going to be gone all day. It's just manners."

"Manners?" Georgette laughed and then considered what Marian said and winced instead. "It would have been better if we'd told them. You're much better at being loved than I am."

"That's because you were alone so long," Marian told Georgette, wrapping her arm around her. "You're still learning. I'll remind Charles for you, if he starts shouting."

"Please do." Georgette laid her hand on Marian's shoulder, suddenly exhausted. "I need to treat Lucy differently. Also Charles. I don't know how to be married."

Marian rubbed Georgette's shoulder as her friend shivered.

"I don't feel well. I—I…I was so focused on finding out who the lover might be, I didn't realize. Marian, if we had come earlier, Morry might have lived."

Georgette felt her knees give a little and Marian helped Georgette to the stairs, ignoring the constables going up and down. Georgette had to be seated before she fell down.

Several more constables had arrived. They were conferring in a circle and then two peeled off to go one way down the street and two peeled off to go the other direction. They started knocking on doors.

What if, Georgette wondered, someone had seen something? What if they'd seen *who* fled the Morry house and if they'd be able to identify the killer? Then it would all be over.

~

JOSEPH AARON

Charles had come into the police station while Joseph had been making himself a list of people who might have had something to do with Polly Siegel's murder. He sighed as he stared down at it and then glanced up at Higgins, waving Charles into a seat.

"None of these names make sense."

"I know," Higgins said. "None of them fit when Polly disappeared either. Barnaby Mustly has a long history of being friendly with the Siegels, including the older boys. It was often seen that he walked with the girl and his wife. He was as *often* seen poking under bushes and examining every inch of ravines when she went missing."

Joseph shoved back his hair and tapped his finger against the paper. "We're *sure* that Mr. Essent was gone when Polly disappeared?"

Higgins nodded. "My superior went to the factory. He interviewed employees. Both those who work with him directly and floor fellows who would have been ignored by Essent. They all agreed that Mr. Essent was in the factory the entire day she disappeared."

"What about tramps or visitors to the town?" Charles asked and then sighed. "Georgette would have laughed at me already for that. Tramps? How would they get Polly into the attic of a house? It has to be someone who could have been around. What about Liam Siegel? Maybe his relationship with Mrs. Essent hadn't really come to an end?"

The constable sighed. "Maybe? I can't see it, myself. Those Siegel boys arrived the same day their sister was missing and they stayed long past everyone else had given up hope looking for her. It isn't just Barnaby Mustly who has a long history of caring about Polly Siegel. Each one of her brothers had the same."

Joseph rubbed the back of his neck. "Call the place where Liam Siegel works anyway. See if they have any record of his attendance around that time and if they can confirm he was there."

Constable Higgins rose and left where Joseph had set up shop.

"I just came by to see if the girls have been here," Charles said. "Georgette took Eddie, Lucy, and Janey to give fruit to the sick children and they've come back but Georgette and Marian are still—"

Joseph shook his head. "I haven't seen them. Knowing them, they're going door to door asking if anyone in the house had murdered Polly Siegel or something else potentially dangerous."

Charles laughed and then the two of them looked at each other again, considering. "You don't think that they—"

"Are actually doing something they probably shouldn't be?" Joseph's head tilted and he started to reply, only Higgins returned.

"We've got a telephone call from the Ely police station," Higgins said. "I believe you'll want to take it."

Joseph rose and followed Higgins, taking the telephone.

"Detective Inspector Aaron?" the voice inquired.

"Yes," Joseph said.

"We've had a murder here, and the two ladies who found the body believe it's connected to one you have there."

Joseph closed his eyes and started counting to ten.

"Sir?"

He had to clear his throat before he could reply. "This wouldn't be Georgette Aaron and Marian Parker?"

The constable on the other end of the call laughed. "I see you know them."

A part of him wanted to reply 'unfortunately,' but instead he said, "I do. Who is dead?"

"A Joan Morry."

Joseph paused. Oh, he was stupid. He should have found her the second he'd learned of her. This was his fault. He'd made a mistake and now a woman was dead. "How did she die?"

"It was strangulation. We thought for a bit that it might be one of your troublemakers, but the doc here thinks she's been gone a bit longer than they've been in Ely and Joan Morry was not—I think—an easy woman to kill. Knowing she's dead, do you think this case is connected to yours?"

"Oh, I'm certain of it."

"Then I guess we better discuss details of what you're doing and what we've found. What do you want me to do with these two?"

"We'll come get them," Joseph sighed.

"Eh," the fellow said almost merrily, "I'll bring them. We've been looking for a bit of a lead here. I'll have my boys gather up what we've found and bring both it and the ladies to you."

Joseph hung up the telephone and admitted to himself he was stupefied and felt even more stupid for feeling so poleaxed.

"Everything all right, sir?" Higgins asked.

"Joan Morry is dead."

Higgins cursed.

"My fiancé and Mrs. Aaron realized we needed to talk her and took it upon themselves to hunt her down. They found the body and were taken in for questioning."

Now Higgins was just staring.

Joseph shook his head and then glanced to where he'd left his uncle. A moment later his gaze met Higgins's and the fellow said, "She seems to be a bit trouble-prone."

Joseph's shout of laughter surprised Higgins, but Joseph only said, "You have no idea, but I am very much afraid you'll learn."

CHAPTER 18

GEORGETTE DOROTHY AARON

*T*here was something very educational, Georgette told herself, about being motored home by a constable who had questioned her about murder. She determined that the only reasonable thing to do was to learn from this experience and put it into a book.

"Joseph is going to wring my neck," Marian muttered. "He'll be right to, but what is worse is when my parents discover what happened—"

"Why should they?"

"My mother has a preternatural ability to look at me and get me to confess, even when I don't wish to reveal all."

"Do you think she'd teach me?" Georgette asked with a sly look.

Marian giggled. "I knew you were expecting before you even told me. I told Joseph so, but he told me I was wishfully dreaming."

"Expecting, Mrs. Aaron? If so," the constable said, "I'd very much prefer that you not be guilty of this crime."

"We aren't," Georgette told him with a gentle tone. "You'll see. Didn't your man say that several neighbors saw a man running away from the house?"

He scoffed. "Yes, they saw a tall-ish, blonde-ish, strong-ish man running down the street. The hat was pulled low and features weren't distinguishable. Perhaps, maybe, they'd be able to identify the fellow again. All that can be said is that perhaps he was scratched by Morry and perhaps he was wearing a suit rather than coveralls."

Georgette snorted and asked, "You don't think that's enough?"

"I think we'll be lucky to find anyone other than you as the killer and no one thinks either of you were strong enough to take on ol' Morry. Her brother said it was laughable that either one of you or both together could have out-muscled his sister. Said, she could have picked you both up with one hand."

"Also, we don't have a motive to have killed Morry. But whoever helped kill and hide Polly Siegel sure had a reason to do so."

The constable glanced at Georgette and Marian and then grumbled under his breath.

BETH BYERS

"A baby," Marian sighed as soon as the constable looked away. "I want to hold her already."

"It could be a boy," Georgette said, watching the world go by.

"But you're training Charles so well to have modern daughters. I feel certain that the universe would be better served by him fathering girls rather than boys."

Georgette placed her hand quite unconsciously over where the baby lay. "He'll be a good father regardless of what we have."

The constable muttered again and Georgette gave him a cheeky grin. She'd caught that statement about modern, interfering women raising a generation of female vipers. He caught her quite unhidden grin and his scowl deepened, drawing a wink from her as well.

"You are not the same in Harper's Hollow as you were in Bard's Crook," Marian told Georgette.

"You two are from Bard's Crook?" He groaned. "I bet you were involved in those murders there, weren't you?"

"The killers were all found," Georgette said mildly. "Clearly, we aren't currently imprisoned, so it wasn't us."

"Mistakes could have been made."

"This is what comes from interfering," Marian told Georgette. "Suddenly it's hard to believe we weren't involved with those crimes."

Georgette's mild reply irritated both Marian and the constable further. "Any fool could see we had nothing to do with Polly Siegel. She's been dead for years, and I only stepped foot in Harper's Hollow this year. Can you blame me for wanting to see justice done to someone who could kill a harmless girl?"

They arrived in Harper's Hollow before teatime and Georgette probably shouldn't have said that they were back in time just as she promised. Even Marian's tolerance for the trouble Georgette attracted seemed to have evaporated.

Georgette waited long enough for Constable Higgins to send her on her way before she meddled more, and then she started walking towards the house.

Marian tucked her arm through Georgette's as they walked. "Are you examining every passing man for a tall-ish, blonde-ish fellow?"

"Of course," Georgette admitted. She nodded towards the tall-ish, blonde-ish man loading a truck in front of the hardware store. "Too young."

"No hat," Marian added. "Not that it couldn't be removed, but why would they?"

Georgette shook her head. There was a tall-ish, blonde-ish man entering the pub. She couldn't help but follow.

"What are you doing?"

"Just watching," Georgette said, taking a seat at the table and ordering a bowl of stew she didn't want. She watched the gents come in and out. There were rather a lot of tall-ish, blonde-ish men when you got right down to it. There was the fellow who was working behind the bar. He worked efficiently, pulling a pint of beer, handing it over, joking with the blonde-ish man who'd ordered a basket of chips. He was a large man in the rotund kind of way and Georgette bet that someone would have mentioned him being fat if they also mentioned him being strongish. There was the blonde-ish man with spectacles sitting down to quite a large steak sandwich. He poured vinegar over his chips and added salt to his sandwich before taking a large bite. For such a slender man, he put the mound of food away rather briskly. There was another fellow at the bar, hunched over a drink. He wasn't, however, sipping slowly. He drank the whole glass of whisky in several gulps and then ordered another.

Georgette shook her head, wondering who the town drunk was when she caught his profile. Why that was Dr. Fowler! She shook her head. Perhaps one of those children he'd misdiagnosed had passed away. Scarlet fever was no easy illness and children died all too often from it.

He ordered another whiskey by lifting his hand, and the sleeve of his shirt pulled back. There were deep scratches on his arm. Why would— An idea occurred to Georgette, a sudden weaving together of ideas really. What if...what if...Georgette shoved back her stew and said, "Come, Marian. I must attend my notes."

Slowly, Dr. Fowler turned and met Georgette's gaze. Had he felt her staring at him? Did he know what she suspected? His gaze narrowed on her, and she wanted to flee. No, Georgette thought, she did not want to flee. She wanted to beat him within an inch of his life, stopping just short of murder because Georgette was not a killer.

Georgette slowly stood, nodded to the doctor, and hurried out of the pub. She strode briskly with Marian having to run to catch up. Tall-ish, blonde-ish, hat pulled low. Georgette shook her head, wondering if she'd gone mad.

Marian followed, demanding an explanation, but Georgette was so busy putting pieces together, she didn't really hear Marian's questions.

Georgette hurried towards the house, feeling a distinct horror that chased her. She rushed inside, seeing Charles rise. He had a worried look on his face, but she couldn't explain her thoughts. She wasn't even sure she could explain her thoughts sensibly. Not when it was the doctor!

"Charles! I need your help." She rushed into his office and began digging through the boxes where they'd set aside paperwork.

"What is it?" he asked. "Is everything well? Is it—"

Joseph had followed them both, but Georgette ignored him and met Charles's gaze, shaking her head. No, it wasn't the baby.

"I think—I think—oh my goodness, I don't want to say it, but it all adds up. Charles! The doctor! He had regular appointments with Yelena Essent. Oh! Where are those bills I found? I found a whole box of house-hold records."

Charles started looking as well, not even eyeing her as if she'd gone mad. This, she thought, was why she loved him. He just helped Georgette dig through the paperwork as Joseph demanded, "The doctor?"

"Joseph! Joseph! Liam said that Yelena had regular

times with one lover. The constable knew Polly had been murdered with one look, but the doctor tried to say it was an accident."

"He also misdiagnosed those children. Georgette, he could just be very bad at his work."

"Here it is," Charles said. He flipped frantically through the pages and then shoved a bill towards Joseph. "If she's right, Mr. Essent paid his wife's lover."

Joseph shook his head. "Where is an old calendar?"

They dug until the found one and then found the date that Polly Siegel disappeared. March 17. Tuesday, March 17. A day wherein Dr. Fowler had sent Mr. Essent a bill for assistance and therapy with Yelena's megrims and hysteria. A Tuesday and Thursday lover. Bills from the doctor for Tuesdays and Thursday. A little girl missing after a Tuesday morning with her friends next door. What *had* Polly Siegel seen that day? It must have been something or why else would she be dead.

Georgette shook her head and then rushed out of the house and down towards the Mustlys' house. She saw Barnaby Mustly sitting on a bench and only waved as she invaded his garden. Georgette was climbing the old ladder to the treehouse.

"What's this?" Mr. Mustly asked Charles, Joseph, and Marian who had followed Georgette.

She didn't answer. She reached the opening in the bottom of the tree house and she slowly crawled inside. It had been cleaned out, but there was still a square box sitting near the window of the treehouse. Georgette took a seat on it and looked towards her house. The view into the master bedroom was as clear as day.

Georgette groaned as Charles crawled through the window. "Take a look."

She didn't want to stay up there any longer. The feel of Polly Siegel in Georgette's house had been... faint. Like a sweet visitor. The feel of Polly Siegel in the treehouse was...it was too strong even if it was just Georgette's imagination. She crawled back down the ladder and before she'd gone halfway, Joseph lifted her down.

"You can see right into the master bedroom."

Mr. Mustly looked between them and then slowly said, "We found a butterfly chrysalis after Anna went inside the house. Polly and I did, and Polly wanted to put it in her treasure box. She crawled up there and puttered around for a good quarter hour before I told her she needed to head home to her mama."

Georgette pressed her fingers to her temples and took in a slow, deep breath. Her hands were shaking and she was certain she was going to sick-up.

"If our timing is right, on a Tuesday in March, Polly Siegel saw Yelena Essent and her lover."

"It seems possible," Joseph said. "And we have the fingerprint on the locket. If it's his fingerprint, we have him! But...it could easily be Yelena Essent's."

Georgette had the soul of a liar, she thought, wondering why they needed to mention the locket. Why be honest with him? She was convinced he was the killer of Polly Siegel. Or, if not the killer, then certainly he conspired to hide her body and knew the truth.

"You need a confession."

"That's what I'm saying," Joseph said. "I can't see us getting it."

"So lie to him."

Joseph frowned and Mr. Mustly surprised them all with a laugh.

"I like her," Mr. Mustly declared as Charles tugged Georgette under the safety of his arm.

"He doesn't need to know where the fingerprint came from, only that you have one and believe it is his. He doesn't need to know that no one could identify him from today in Ely—only that he was seen. In fact, he has to know he billed Mr. Essent. Tell him you found the bills, took a sketch of him to Ely, and that you know it was him."

"You lie all too easily," Charles told Georgette. He didn't, however, sound bothered.

"You know that, darling. You do pay me to do it."

CHAPTER 19

GEORGETTE DOROTHY AARON

*I*n the morning, Charles said, "Have you considered that we could leave this all to Joseph and escape to Brussels?"

Georgette was sitting her with tea, eyes closed, realizing that her stomach did *not* want her tea. It was possible that her heart was breaking. Was the baby doing this to her? She'd noticed changes to the feelings of her chest as she dressed. She had been, she thought, rather more emotional than usual.

But...but her tea? Georgette couldn't abide the thought. She cracked her eyelids and asked, almost waspishly, "Have you considered that we bought a house that needs expensive renovations, and you own a business that you've neglected?"

Charles reached out and trailed a finger down her arm. "So we aren't being imaginative today?"

Georgette groaned, jerked her arm away from him, and said, "I might sick up. The smell of my tea is making me want to sick up." She had to admit that her confession had ended on a wail. She had gone full-mad, she thought. "I can't survive without tea."

Charles carefully examined her as she gave him her dourest look through her lashes.

"Your child is a demon."

He bit back a laugh and she might have growled. She wasn't quite sure, but she was *almost* certain she growled at him. At which point, he was no longer able to hold back his laugh.

"What if I were to get you some ginger tea? I believe that ginger tea, mint, and chamomile might see you through."

"I need it," Georgette whined. "I can't just drink chamomile and mint. I wonder if I could mix black tea and ginger tea."

"You could try," Charles said gently. "You'll stay in the house while I go?"

"I swear," Georgette told him, crossing her finger over her heart, "I will not leave this house. Surely, Joseph is rounding up the doctor the moment he leaves?"

Charles pressed a kiss to her forehead. "It seems likely."

"Wonderful," Georgette said, trying not to cry over tea. "I'll just work on my book and not think of tea or food or any sort of anything."

He paused and then nodded. "See that you do." He pressed a kiss to her forehead again and then whispered, "We'll find a tea for you. It will be all right. I promise our baby is not a demon and as the years pass, will even join you for a cuppa often."

Georgette pressed a kiss to his chin. "You turn an excellent phrase and promise a bright future, as I've already discovered."

Joseph stuck his head into the breakfast room and said, "Higgins is here to help me take everything back to the police office. We'll be going after Dr. Fowler before luncheon, I hope."

Marian had not arrived in the breakfast room, and it seemed that Joseph was bypassing breakfast. Georgette wondered if she might curl up in her bed once again. The idea was appealing even though she'd slept far too long. Was this what growing a baby was like? Georgette found herself wishing desperately for her mother. She yawned and pushed her tea back.

Then again, Georgette thought, her tea did provide her that first necessary burst of energy. If she wasn't able to choke it down, would she be lethargic and useless without it? Georgette had a deep frown on her face when she made her way to the library to write.

She was not going to be a victim of no tea. She was not going to lose more days to honeymooning or bodies or investigations. She was going to dive into her book and it wouldn't be as black as her mood.

Georgette settled back in the most comfortable chair she could find and sipped her *water* as she returned to her story. She had to read it through again, having completely lost the thread of the tale.

Once feeling in her spine had disappeared, Georgette took her dogs to the garden, pacing until she'd recovered all feeling in her limbs. When she returned to the library, she found Janey lying on the floor near the desk where Georgette was working with a copy of *Little Women.* Georgette noted the fresh cool water and the plate of biscuits, and told Janey she was an angel.

To Georgette's surprise, hunger had returned. What if she were able to eat a biscuit and not feel sick? Could she dare a pot of tea then? Georgette broke off a piece of the biscuit, popped it in her mouth and noticed the dogs were gone.

"Where are the pups?"

"It's past luncheon," Janey said. "Charles said it would be all right for Marian to take them to the wood and run them. He left for your tea and to ensure that Dr. Fowler was both figuratively and literally behind bars. What does that mean?"

Georgette explained, hoping that Dr. Fowler was realizing the depth of his trouble, but he wasn't going to take her mind over anymore. The story was scratching at the edges of Georgette's mind, so she sank right back into the writing, the typewriter click-clacking as she sped through her thoughts. It was pouring out of her in a way that was nearly magical. It wasn't so much that she was writing it as she was simply transcribing the scenes playing out in her mind.

She rubbed her brow as she loaded another sheet

of paper into the typewriter and then sipped her water, regretting immensely that it was not tea.

"Maybe you'll be all right, little one," she muttered. She stretched her neck and her side, and realized that there was a creak in the hallway. Georgette frowned, quite certain that Eunice had gone out to work in the kitchen garden.

It was just an old house settling, Georgette thought, but there was a creak again. The protective mama came out in Georgette. There was something furtive to the slow creaking of the wood that sent Georgette's instincts screaming.

She hissed, "Janey, under the desk."

To Georgette's surprise the little girl scrambled under without a word. Georgette glanced down, wishing the dogs were there. If they had been, she'd know if it was just the house moving or something else.

Georgette shivered, feeling certain that someone had come into the house despite no confirmation from the dogs. There was no way Joseph had returned. Not yet. Charles wouldn't lurk. None of them who lived there would linger in the hallway, quietly.

Slowly Georgette glanced around. Where was the convenient fireplace poker? Where was the silver letter opener, sharp and easily accessible? Georgette heard the creak again and with it this time, the distinct sound of a footstep.

The door to the library opened and Georgette looked up in surprise, pretending to not be bothered in the least at the sight of Dr. Fowler! Where was

Joseph? Where was Eunice or Eddie or Lucy? Though Georgette's mind shifted again. This was a killer. She wanted Eunice, Eddie, and Lucy in the distance safe and sound. If only Janey were as well.

"Dr. Fowler, if I am correct?" Georgette rose and crossed to him, holding out her hand as though all was well. His smile was too smooth and too cold for her comfort, but she greeted him as though she were happy to see him.

"Oh, I am sorry I missed the door. I confess, I quite dive into my own mind when I am writing."

"Yes," Dr. Fowler said, stepping closer and forcing her to back up. She tried to casually return to her desk, waving him to the seat in front of it. "I'd heard you write frivolous little tales."

If she hadn't been terrified, the condescending, mocking tone would have filled her with fury.

"Frivolous indeed," Georgette said merrily, trying not to sick up. "I did just spend the entirety of my morning wondering how to describe a dress's embroidery. How much is too much, do you know?"

"Any description is too much. But I'm not one for *novels*."

Scared or not, Georgette just thought she might invite him to take his opinions elsewhere.

"I fear Charles has stepped out," Georgette told Dr. Fowler. "Did you want me to have him stop by your office?"

"Who knows when he'll be back? Quite late, I imagine."

"Possibly," Georgette said. "Though I doubt it. He

tends to stay near home and work while he's here. I'm sorry you missed him."

"Oh, I missed him quite purposefully. I understand you saw me in Ely?"

Georgette's distinct confusion made Dr. Fowler pause, but then he realized what he'd said. No, she hadn't seen him in Ely. But, he'd just admitted to being there.

"You did go to Ely?" he demanded.

"I'm looking for help for my house," Georgette lied. Her hands were shaking, and she grasped her chair. *Where* was Joseph? "People here feel that this house is haunted."

"I wouldn't be surprised. By a sleuthing, spying brat, no doubt."

Georgette took the seat behind her desk, still trying to pretend all was normal, and gestured to Dr. Fowler to take his own. "Didn't you like Polly? The poor thing. It was my understanding that everyone loved her."

"She was useless." Dr. Fowler leaned back and crossed his hands over his stomach. "She was a drain on her mother and those around her. The world is better without those like her. Why did you really go to Ely?"

It was obvious he wasn't going to leave and Georgette decided to try truth instead. Maybe she could fluster him enough to let Janey escape and go for help.

So she answered truthfully. "If anyone knew what happened the day Polly Siegel died, it would have been Morry."

173

Dr. Fowler started, then a victorious smile took over his handsome face. "Another useless old woman who should have been put out to pasture."

"Well, you did that, didn't you?" Georgette said calmly. Janey took hold of Georgette's ankle, squeezing, but Georgette didn't stop. "You killed Morry and Polly. The girl saw you that day, didn't she? Saw you and didn't understand about being quiet."

"As I said, she was useless."

Georgette swallowed dryly. "Why are you here, really? You know I didn't see you in Ely."

"I had heard you had," Dr. Fowler admitted. "I'd heard you were brought back in the constable's auto. You were there and then suddenly questions were being asked about me. I saw your look in the pub. I assumed you had realized and with you gone, who will testify at the trial?"

"No," Georgette said, "it wasn't because of Ely. You were too greedy."

"Greedy?"

"You billed Mr. Essent for your visits. Did you and his wife laugh over how he paid you?"

"We did," Dr. Fowler replied. "Of course we did. What does that matter?"

"Joseph has the bills, of course. He'll know where you've gone. I'm sure he's looking for you. How long will it take for them to arrive?"

"They won't find me here," Dr. Fowler said smoothly. "I've an auto hidden. I'll be working at the university researching when they come for me. Librarians saw me arrive. I asked to be left alone.

They'll find me there, pouring over my notes. Witnesses to my presence. Easy, easy."

Georgette's mind was searching. He was far too calm about what he had done, and what he intended to do to her. No remorse whatsoever. What could she do to save herself, and more importantly Janey?

"You shouldn't have billed him for the day you murdered Polly Siegel," she said, giving away one of their pieces of evidence. "You shouldn't have been here regularly with Yelena Essent. Her other lovers knew she had a lover in those times. The evidence is mountainous."

It worked. A look of slow horror crossed his face.

"They know it was you."

He slowly cracked his neck, his gaze never leaving Georgette. "Did you tell them?"

"Scotland Yard detectives don't need a small-town wife to do their work."

"Then why did you get involved?" He said it as an accusation.

"Polly Siegel haunts me," Georgette said. "I can't get her out of mind. I feel like I see her in the corner of my eye whenever I walk down a hall alone or turn a corner in this house."

He started, eyes wide and jumping so much that she thought he wasn't as remorseless as she'd thought. He might have been driven mad by what he'd done.

"Does she haunt you too?"

"Shut up!"

"Do you see her when you close your eyes? Dead on the floor? Do you see what you did to her?"

"I said shut up!"

Georgette felt Janey move at her feet and hoped that the girl wasn't going to reveal herself. "Why are you here?"

"To silence you."

Georgette laughed. "Silence me? From what? Saying that you killed Morry? They don't need me for that."

"They don't know anything if you die. It's all guesses and supposition. I'm a long-standing, well-respected doctor in this town who has witnesses that I was elsewhere when you die. They'll assume your killer is Polly's killer. They'll be right of course, but they won't realize it was me."

Georgette laughed again. "Well, not *well-respected*. The first thing I heard here was how you endangered all those children with your mistakes. Do you even have clients left in this town? Is that why you need to pretend to be researching elsewhere?"

He rose, his face white with rage. "I said to shut up." It wasn't yelled. It was a cool, cold order.

Georgette stood, refusing to let him strangle her in the chair as he'd done to Morry. No, she was going to do all she could to fight him, and angering him might cause him to make a mistake. She laughed at him. "The foolish doctor who couldn't even identify scarlet fever."

"Shut up!"

"The idiot who murdered his own lover while he murdered their baby."

"That baby could have been a good three or four men's."

"But it could have been yours. Did you intend to kill her or are you just as stupid as I think you are?"

His gaze narrowed on Georgette and he went far too still. "I will enjoy killing you the most, I think."

He grabbed hold of the desk where Georgette had been writing and turned it over. Georgette screamed, horrified that he'd found Janey.

He saw her and screamed himself. "Polly! Bloody hell, Polly!"

Janey scrambled to Georgette. The doctor took in the sight of Janey hiding behind Georgette and lunged, tripping to face-plant onto the floor.

"Run, Georgie!" Janey screamed.

They grasped hands and darted through the house with Georgette calling for her dogs. They ran out the front door just as Dr. Fowler reached the doorway of the library and came down the steps.

"Help! Anna!" Georgette screamed, hoping to lead them away from anyone she loved. She noted Charles's missing auto and wished desperately he hadn't left for tea. "Barnaby!"

They rushed towards the Mustly house just as Marian and Lucy rounded the end of Persephone Street. Neither Georgette nor Janey slowed as they ran. They were calling for help and Marian and Lucy started forward with the dogs racing along.

Janey was screaming for her sister with Marian only a step behind Lucy. As they threw themselves at each other, Georgette looked back and saw Barnaby

Mustly, shovel in hand, strike out at Dr. Fowler with a hard, swift blow.

Dr. Fowler hadn't seen Mr. Mustly in the shadows, and with a horrifying crunch the blow sent him flying off of his feet. Georgette kept moving, refusing to let go of Janey's hand as they landed in Marian and Lucy's arms.

Lucy took possession of her sister and they all looked back to see Barnaby Mustly set down his shovel and stare down at Dr. Fowler.

"I—" Barnaby leaned down and turned Dr. Fowler's head, fingers touching his throat. "I think he's dead."

His wife approached from the house. "Call for the constables, Anna. I've killed Polly's murderer."

Georgette refused to look or to see. She pressed her face into Marian as her friend gasped. "I can't believe he's dead."

Georgette pulled away and grabbed Janey and Lucy, hauling them farther down the street with the order of, "Don't look!"

"We've seen dead people before," Janey told Georgette almost callously. "It won't bother us. He was a bad man. He deserved to die."

"Even still," Georgette muttered. "Even still."

When they were too far away to see the expression on the dead doctor's face, Georgette pulled the girls with her to the side of the street and sat down on the edge. It took Georgette a moment to catch her breath and calm the terror before she glanced at Janey. "What did you do?"

"Tied his shoelaces together."

Georgette blinked. Her dogs surrounded her and Georgette pulled Dorcas into her lap and let Bea lick her face frantically. Susan was pawing at Janey, who sat down next to Georgette.

"I used to do it to Eddie all the time," Janey announced proudly. "I knew it would slow him down. I thought if he was just visiting, you could blame me for being young and silly. If he wasn't, I didn't think it would hurt."

"It saved us," Georgette told Janey, wrapping her arm around the child. "You precious creature. You saved us."

Anna Mustly returned from her telephone call and poor Joseph and Constable Higgins arrived. They must have sped through the village to reach them. Joseph rushed to Georgette and Marian while Constable Higgins approached Barnaby Mustly.

"Why did he come to the house?" Joseph demanded. "I was told he was in some college's library."

"He heard about Georgette going to Ely and thought she saw him." Janey's piping little voice seemed to draw even more attention to the horror of what had occurred.

Joseph's jaw dropped as he turned his attention to Georgette again.

"Our gazes did meet in the pub," Georgette admitted. "I thought I was better at hiding my thoughts. My reaction must have been enough once he heard about Ely. He thought I saw him and he was removing a witness. I am not sure he was entirely sane," Georgette added. "He was so cool about planning my murder that it seemed an act in a play."

Janey laughed. "You scared him when you said you were haunted by Polly."

"He must have been haunted as well," Marian told Georgette. "You are so good at seeing into the hearts of people."

Georgette shivered. She didn't feel seeing into anyone's heart was one of her gifts. She frowned, staring towards where Barnaby Mustly and the constables were talking over Fowler's body.

She was sick to her stomach and desperately wanted her husband with whatever tea he'd acquired. Residual terror was racking her and the blithe, sweet Janey was laughing despite the dead man down the street.

"What you need," Marian announced, "is a cup of tea and your bed."

What she got, however, was Charles's auto screeching to a stop and him almost falling out from behind the wheel, followed by Eddie. Charles darted into the thick of things, taking in the sight of Barnaby Mustly handing over his shovel, the dead Dr. Fowler, and Georgette half-gagging on the side of the street.

Georgette found herself being scooped into Charles's arms, carried to her bed, and placed on a stack of pillows that Lucy propped up. Janey climbed into the bed, ignoring Charles's protest. Eddie, at least, took one of the chairs near the bed.

"She needs rest."

"It's lunchtime," Janey said. "If she sleeps now, she'll

be up all night with bad dreams. Read to us."

Janey was joined by Lucy and Marian. Eunice arrived only minutes later with ginger tea and a stack of books, and Charles gave in begrudgingly as he clasped Georgette's hand tight.

"I am sorry I am being such a wilting flower," Georgette told him. "Please don't worry."

His look said she was dim if she thought he wouldn't.

"I'm sure it's just the baby," Marian said, patting Georgette's hand.

"Read to her," Eunice ordered Charles. "Diving into another world will cleanse all of our minds."

Rather than leaving, Eunice took her seat next to the bed as the dogs leapt onto the covers and joined Georgette. The innocence of Beth, Jo, Amy, and Meg chased Georgette into sleep despite Janey's dire warning.

"Is Mr. Mustly going to be arrested?" Georgette asked Joseph the next morning.

Joseph paused long enough for her to worry. "Dr. Fowler was trying to kill you. Mr. Mustly saved your life. He'll be fine."

"Is he upset?"

"He seems to feel as though justice had been served though he swears he only intended to incapacitate Fowler. His only worry was being taken to prison and leaving his wife alone."

"Does the Siegel family know?"

"The fiery one cursed a storm that he wasn't the one to murder Fowler. The one who'd been lovers with Mrs. Essent seemed sick at what we'd learned, but they were mostly relieved. Polly's funeral is going to happen tomorrow."

Georgette closed her eyes, leaning back with her tea. Anna Mustly had brought more of her cinnamon and orange tea over, and Georgette breathed it in. The scent warmed her lungs. She sipped. Her stomach had not returned to normal despite sleeping the horror away. She'd woken only once and found herself wrapped tightly in Charles's arms.

"I stayed in the house," Georgette told Charles as she opened her eyes and took her tea. "I was working on my book when he showed up."

"So I understand," he said. "We've added three children and four cats to our little household. I believe we shall have to add quite a large, fierce dog."

Georgette spread marmalade over her toast. "Well, it's not like we're going to find another body in the attic or under the hedges."

"I think we can all agree," Joseph told Georgette simply, "that you attract trouble. Marian will need one of those fierce creatures as well. You two seem to be sisters in trouble."

"Innocent," Georgette said. "I declare myself innocent."

"Georgette," Charles said, lifting her hand and pressing a kiss to each of her fingers. "Happily ever afters require safeguarding and nurturing. Perhaps they also require protection."

"Is this our happily ever after?" Georgette asked him.

"Well." Charles pressed a kiss on the center of her palm, entirely unbothered by their audience. "I am happy. And it is after, so it must be."

ONCE AGAIN, the goddess Atë leaned back in satisfaction. Perhaps, she thought, the little man in the north wasn't worthy of her attention quite yet. After all, Joseph wasn't wrong that Georgette attracted trouble. And Charles wasn't wrong that protection would be required in the coming days. Really, Atë thought, small towns were so much more fun than sprawling cities. Delightful rivers flowed through the countryside, blessed by Apollo or one of those other fools. Hera delighted in the families. But under the layers of sweet and wholesome, or hatred and greed, that lovely thing—mischief—abounded.

The End

HULLO FRIENDS! Once again, it's my chance to tell you how much I appreciate you reading my books and giving me a chance. If you wouldn't mind, I would be so grateful for a review.

· · ·

THE SEQUEL to this book is available now. If you want book updates, you could also follow me on Facebook.

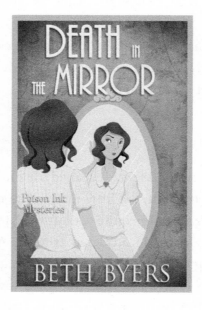

September 1937

Georgette Dorothy Aaron is expecting a bundle of joy, focusing on updating her house, writing books, and enjoying her family. What she's not doing is meddling. She's not sticking her nose in other people's business. She's not writing books about her neighbors. She's determined to turn over a new leaf and slide right back into the safety of being a wallflower.

Georgette, however, gets stuck on her book, sick of the smell of drying paint, and decides to take a ramble. When she stops to check herself in the mirror, she doesn't expect to see someone *else* in the reflection. Nor does she expect what happens next.

Order your copy here.

A new paranormal 1920s series is coming soon.

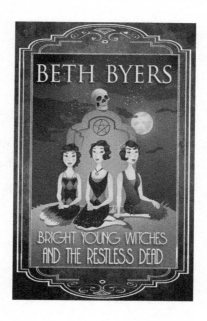

April 1922

When the Klu Klux Klan appears at the door of the Wode sisters, they decide it's time to visit the ancestral home in England.

With squabbling between the sisters, it takes them too long to realize that their new friend is being haunted. Now they'll have to set aside their fight, discover just why their friend is being haunted, and what they're going to do about it. Will they rid their friend of the ghost and out themselves as witches? Or will they look away?

Join the Wode as they rise up and embrace just who and what they are in this newest historical mystery adventure.

Order your copy here.

THERE IS ALSO a new 1920s series about two best friends, written by one of my best friends and I. If you'd like to check it out, keep on flipping for the first chapter.

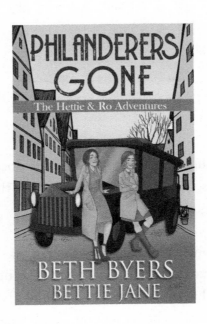

July 1922

If there's one thing to draw you together, it's shared misery.

Hettie and Ro married manipulative, lying, money-grubbing pigs. Therefore, they were instant friends. When those philandering dirtbags died, they found themselves the subjects of a murder investigation. Did they kill their husbands? No. Did they joke about it? Maybe. Do they need to find the killer before the crime is pinned on them? They do!

Join Hettie and Ro and their growing friendship as they delve into their own lives to find a killer, a best friend, and perhaps a brighter new outlook.

Order your copy here.

Christmas Madness: A Short Story Anthology

Hijinks & Murder

Love & Murder

A Zestful Little Murder (coming soon)

A Murder Most Odd (coming soon)

Nearly A Murder (coming soon)

THE POISON INK MYSTERIES

Death By the Book

Death Witnessed

Death by Blackmail

Death Misconstrued

Deathly Ever After

Death in the Mirror

A Merry Little Death

Death Between the Pages

THE 2ND CHANCE DINER MYSTERIES

(This series is complete.)

Spaghetti, Meatballs, & Murder

Cookies & Catastrophe

Poison & Pie

Double Mocha Murder

Cinnamon Rolls & Cyanide

Tea & Temptation

Donuts & Danger

Scones & Scandal

Lemonade & Loathing

Wedding Cake & Woe

Honeymoons & Honeydew

The Pumpkin Problem

THE HETTIE & RO ADVENTURES

cowritten with Bettie Jane

(This series is complete.)

Philanderer Gone

Adventurer Gone

Holiday Gone

Aeronaut Gone

ALSO BY AMANDA A. ALLEN

THE MYSTIC COVE MOMMY MYSTERIES

Bedtimes & Broomsticks

Runes & Roller Skates

Banshees and Babysitters

Hobgoblins and Homework

Christmas and Curses

Valentines & Valkyries

THE RUE HALLOW MYSTERIES

Hallow Graves

Hungry Graves

Lonely Graves

Sisters and Graves

Yule Graves

Fated Graves

Ruby Graves

THE INEPT WITCHES MYSTERIES

(co-written with Auburn Seal)

(This series is complete.)

Inconvenient Murder

Moonlight Murder

Bewitched Murder

Presidium Vignettes (with Rue Hallow)

Prague Murder

Paris Murder

Murder By Degrees

PREVIEW OF PHILANDERER GONE

CHAPTER ONE

*T*he house was one of those ancient stone artisan-crafted monstrosities that silently, if garishly, announced out and out *buckets* of bullion, ready money, the green, call it what you would, these folks were simply rolling in the good life. The windows were stained glass with roses and stars. The floor was wide-planked dark wood that was probably some Egyptian wood carried by camel and horse through deserts to the house.

Hettie hid a smirk when a very tall, beautiful, uniformed man slid through the crowd and leaned down, holding a tray of champagne and cocktails in front of her with a lascivious gaze. She wasn't quite sure if he appreciated the irony of his status as human art for the party, or if he embraced it and the opportunity it gave him to romance bored wives.

She was, very much, a bored wife. Or, maybe disillusioned was the better word. She took yet another flute of champagne and curled into the chair, pulling up her legs, leaving her shoes behind.

The sight of her husband laughing uproariously with a drink in each hand made her want to skip over to him and toss her champagne into his face. He had been drinking and partying so heavily, he'd become yellowed. The dark circles under his eyes emphasized his utter depravity. Or, then again, perhaps that was the disillusionment once again. Which came first? The depravity or the dark circles?

"Fiendish brute," Hettie muttered, lifting her glass to her own, personal animal. Her husband, Harvey, wrapped his arm around another bloke, laughing into his face so raucously the poor man must have felt as though he'd stepped into a summer rainstorm.

"Indeed," a woman said and Hettie flinched, biting back a gasp to twist in the chair and see who had overheard her.

What a shocker! If Hettie had realized that anyone was around instead of a part of that drunken sea of flesh, she'd have insulted him non-verbally. It was quite satisfying to speak her feelings out loud. Heaven knew he deserved every ounce of criticism. She had nothing against dancing, jazz, cocktails, or adventure. She did, however, have quite a lot against Harvey.

He had discovered her in Quebec City. Or rather he'd discovered she was an heiress and then pretended to *discover* her. He'd written her love letters and poems, praising her green eyes, her red hair, and her pale skin as though being nearly dead-girl white were something to be envied. He'd made her feel beautiful even though she tended towards the plump, and he'd seemed oblivious to the spots she'd been dealing with on her chin and jawline through all of those months.

A fraud in more ways than Hettie could count, he'd spent the subsequent months prostrating himself at her feet, romancing her, wearing down her defenses until she'd strapped on the old white dress and discovered she'd gotten a drunken, spoiled, rude, lying ball and chain.

"Do you hate him too?" Hettie asked, wondering if she were commiserating with one of her husband's lovers. She would hardly be surprised.

"Oh so much so," the woman said. Her gaze met Hettie's and then she snorted. "Such a wart. Makes everything a misery. It's a wonder that no one has clocked him over the back of the head yet."

Hettie shocked herself with a laugh, totally unprepared to instantly adore one of her husband's mistresses, but they seemed to share more than one thing in common. "If only!"

She lifted her glass in toast to the woman, who grinned and lifted her own back. "Cheers, darling."

"So, are you one of his lovers?" the woman asked after they had drunk.

"Wife," Hettie said and the woman's gaze widened.

"Wife? I hardly think so."

"Believe me," Hettie replied. "I wish it wasn't so."

"As his wife," the woman said with a frown, "I fear I must dispute your claim."

Hettie's gaze narrowed and she glanced back at Harvey. His blonde hair had been pomaded back, but some hijinks had caused the seal on the pomade to shift and it was flopping about in greasy lanks. He had a drink in front of him and the man he'd been molesting earlier had one as well. The two clanked their glasses together and guzzled the cocktails. Harvey leaned into the man and they both laughed raucously.

"Idiot," the woman said. "Look at him gulping down a drink that anyone with taste would have sipped. The blonde one, he must be yours?"

Hettie nodded with disgust and grimaced. "Unfortunately, yes, the blond wart with the pomade gone wrong is my unfortunate ball and chain. So the other fool is yours?"

The woman laughed. "I suppose I sounded almost jealous. I wasn't, you know. I'd have been happy if Leonard was yours."

"Alas, my fate has been saddled with yon blonde horse, Harvey."

They grinned at each other and then the other woman held out her hand. "Ro Lavender, so pleased to meet someone with my same ill-fate. Makes me feel less alone."

Hettie looked at that fiend of hers, then held out her own hand. "Hettie Hughes. I thought Leonard's last name was Ripley."

"Oh, it is," Ro said. "I try not to tie myself to his wagon unless it benefits me. At the bank, for instance."

Ro was a breath of fresh air. Hettie decided nothing else would do except to keep her close. "Shall we be bosom friends?" Hettie asked.

"I just read that book," Ro said. "Do you love it as well?"

"I'm Canadian," Hettie replied, standing to twine her arm through Ro's. "Of course I've read it. Anne, Green Gables, Diana, Gilbert, Marilla, and Prince Edward Island were fed to me with milk as a babe. Only those of us with a fiendish brute for a husband can truly understand the agony of another. How did you get caught?"

"Family pressure. We were raised together. Quite close friends over the holidays, but I never knew the real him until after."

Hettie winced. "Love letters for me," she said disgustedly. "You'd think modern women such as ourselves wouldn't have been quite so..."

"Stupid," Ro replied, tucking her bobbed hair behind her ear.

The laughter from the crowd around the table became too much to hear anything and Hettie raised her voice to ask, "Why are we here? Shall we escape into the nighttime?"

"Let's go to Prince Edward Island," Ro joked. "Is it magical there? I've always wanted to go."

"I've never been," Hettie admitted, "but I have a sudden desperate need. Let's flee. You know they won't miss us until their fathers insist they arrive with their respectable wives on their arms."

"Or," Ro joked, "I could murder yours and you could murder mine, and we could create our freedom. If our families want respectable, I would definitely respect a woman that could rid herself of these monsters."

"That sounds lovely. Until we can plan our permanent freedom, I suppose our best option is simply to disappear into the night."

Ro lifted her glass in salute and sipped.

Hettie set aside her champagne flute, slipped on her shoes, and then turned to face her husband, who had pulled Mrs. Stone, the obvious trollop, into his lap and was kissing her extravagantly. Hettie scrunched up her nose and gagged a little. Mrs. Stone had been in Nathan Brighton's lap last week.

"She slept with Leonard too," Ro informed Hettie with an even tone.

Hettie reveled in the camaraderie she found in Ro's resigned tone. "Have you met Mr. Stone?"

Ro nodded. "He doesn't realize. He's not the type of man to be cuckolded like this. So…overtly. Have you heard of the marriage act they've proposed?"

Hettie nodded with little doubt that her eyes had brightened like that of a child at Christmas. "I will be there on the very first day. If Harvey had any idea, any at all, he'd be rolling over in his future grave. The money's mine, you know? My aunt never liked Harvey and she tied up my money tightly. He gets what he wants because it's easier to give it to him than listen to him whine, but he won't get a half-penny from me the day I can file divorce papers. They say it's going to go through."

"I couldn't care less about the money," Ro replied. "Though my money is coming from a still-living aunt. Leonard has enough, I suppose, but his eye is definitely on Aunt Bette's fortune."

"So," Hettie joked, "he needs to go before she does."

Ro choked on a laugh and cough-laughed so hard she was wiping away tears.

"Darling!" Harvey hollered across the room. "We're going down to Leonard's yacht. You can get yourself home, can't you?"

Hettie closed her eyes for a moment before answering. "Of course I can. Don't fall in." She crossed her fingers so only Ro could see. Ro's laugh made Hettie grin at Harvey. He gave her a bit of a confused look. Certainly he had shouted his exit with the hope she wouldn't scold him. Foolish man! She'd welcome him moving into Mrs. Stone's bed permanently and leaving his wife behind.

The handsome servant from earlier picked up Hettie's abandoned glass and shot her a telling, not quite disapproving look.

"Oh ho," Hettie said, making sure the man heard her. "We've been overheard."

"We've been eavesdropped," Ro agreed. Then with a lifted brow to the human art serving champagne, she said, "Boy, our husbands are aware of our lack of love. There's no chance for blackmail here."

"Does your aunt feel the same?" he asked insinuatingly.

Hettie stiffened, but Ro simply laughed. "Do you think she hasn't heard the tale of that lush Leonard? She's written me stiff upper lip letters. Watch your step and your mouth or you'll lose your position despite your pretty face. It doesn't matter how you feel, only how you look. No one is paying you to think."

The servant flushed and bowed deeply, shooting them both a furious expression before backing away silently.

"Cheeky lad," Hettie muttered. "You scolded him furiously. Are you sure you weren't letting out your rage on the poor fellow?"

"Cheeky yes," Ro agreed. She placed a finger on her lip as she considered Hettie's question and then agreed. "Too harsh as well. I suppose I would need to apologize if he didn't threaten to blackmail me."

"But pretty," they said nearly in unison, then laughed as the servant overhead them and gave them a combined sultry glance.

"No, no, boyo," Ro told him. "Toddle off now, darling. We've had quite our fill of philandering, reckless men. You've missed your window." Ro's head cocked as she glanced Hettie over. "Shall we?"

"Shall we what, love?"

Ro grinned wickedly. "Shall we be bosom friends then? Soul sisters after one shared breath?"

"Let's," Hettie nodded. "As the man I thought was

my soulmate was an utter disaster, I'll take a soul sister as a replacement."

They sent a servant to summon Hettie's driver. "I was thinking of going to a bottle party later. At a bath house? That might distract us."

Hettie cocked her head as she considered. "Harvey *does* expect me to go home."

Ro lifted her brows and waited.

"So we must, of course, disillusion him as perfectly as he has me."

"There we go! It's only fair," Ro cheered, shaking her hands over her head. "I have been considering a trip to the Paris fashion salons."

"Yes," Hettie immediately agreed, knowing it would enrage Harvey, who preferred her tucked away in case he wanted her. "We should linger in Paris or swing over to Spain."

"Oooh, Spain!"

"Italy," Hettie suggested, just to see if Ro would agree.

"Yes!"

"Russia?"

Ro paused. "Perhaps Cote d'Azur? Egypt? Somewhere warmer. I always think of snow when I think of Russia, and I only like it with cocoa and sleigh rides. Perhaps only one or two days a year."

"Agreed—" Hettie trailed off, eyes wide, as she saw Mrs. Stone enthusiastically kiss the cheeky servant from earlier and then adjust her coat. She winked at Hettie on the way out, caring little that both of them knew Mrs. Stone would be climbing into Harvey's bed later. Or, perhaps it was Harvey who would be climbing into *Mr.* Stone's bed. "Is her husband really blind to it?"

"Oh yes," Ro laughed. "He's quite a bit older you know, and even more old-fashioned than my grandfather. He's Victorian through and through. He probably has a codicil in the will about her remarrying. The type of things that cuts her off if she doesn't remain true to him. Especially since he's in his seventies, and she's thirty? Perhaps?"

Hettie shook her head. "They have a rather outstanding blackberry wine here," she said, putting Mrs. Stone out of her mind. "Shall we—ah—borrow a bottle or two?"

Ro nodded and walked across to the bar. She dug through the bottles and pulled out a full bottle of blackberry wine, another of gin, and a third of a citrus liqueur. "Hopefully someone will think to bring good mixers." She handed one of the bottles to Hettie before tucking one under each arm.

The butler eyed them askance as they asked for their coats.

"Don't worry, luv," Ro told the butler. "Your master doesn't mind."

None of them believed that whopper of a lie, but Ro's cheerful proclamation made it seem acceptable.

"Thief," Hettie hissed innocently as her driver, Peterson, opened the door for them and they dove inside. She struggled with the cork and then asked, "Are we going nude or shall we grab bathing costumes?"

"My brother-in-law lives with us," Ro said, looking disgusted, "I'll be going nude before I go back and face that one. Look—" Her head cocked as the black cab sped up. "I think that's him! We can rush back to collect my bathing costume before he returns to the house."

"I'm a bit too round to want to go full starkers."

"The men love the curves," Ro told her. "If you wanted to step out on your Harvey, you'd need to up the attitude and cast a come hither gaze."

"Like this?" Hettie asked, attempting one but feeling as though she must look like she had something in her eye.

"Like this," Ro countered, glancing at Hettie out of the corner of her eye. "I'm thinking of a really nice plate of biscuits."

Hettie tried it and Ro bit back a laugh. "Are you angry with the biscuits?"

"Let me try imagining cakes. I do prefer a lemon cake." Hettie glanced at Ro out of the corner of her eye, imagining a heavily iced lemon cake, and then smiled just a little.

"No, no," Ro said, showing Hettie again what to do.

"Oh! I know." Hettie imagined the divorce act that Parliament was considering.

"Yes! Now you've got it! Was it a box of chocolates?"

Hettie confessed, sending Ro into a bout of laughter and tears that saw them all the way to Hettie's hotel room. From her hotel room to Ro's house, there were random bursts of giggles and stray tears. Once they reached to bath house, Ro said, "I'll be drinking to that divorce act tonight. Possibly for the rest of my life."

"If it frees me," Hettie told Ro dryly, "I'd paper my house with a copy of it to celebrate those who saved us from a fate I should have known better than to fall into."

ORDER YOUR COPY HERE.